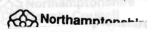
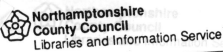

Please return or renew this item by the last date shown.
You may renew items (unless they have been requested
by another customer) by telephoning, writing to or
calling in at the library.   100% recycled paper.   BKS 1

Death Launch

When children's author, Micky Douglas, invites Maddy Grey to launch his latest book, he has no idea he's inviting trouble. Maddy, well-known hostess of the successful children's TV show *Kid's World*, isn't as popular with her colleagues as she is with her adoring young audience. In fact, she's managed to alienate quite a number of her acquaintances, some of whom are finding their very livelihood and future happiness threatened by her vindictive behaviour. It seems a lot of people have very good reasons for wishing Maddy Grey dead.

So when her body turns up after the launch, the police have quite a list of suspects. But who killed Maddy Grey? Was it her ex-lover and co-host? Or her own daughter? The *Kids' World* producer—or his wife? The over-emotional writer of teenage novels whom Maddy threatened to destroy? Or perhaps the journalist whose lover Maddy seduced from her. It might be her agent, or the TV newsreader, or one of the family who runs the bookshop where the launch took place.

The killer is determined to cover any tracks and Micky, realizing that he himself has been responsible for one of the following deaths, is determined to bring a murderer to justice.

ANNE INFANTE

Death Launch

THE CRIME CLUB
An Imprint of HarperCollins *Publishers*

First published in Great Britain in 1993
by The Crime Club, an imprint of
HarperCollins Publishers, 77–85 Fulham Palace Road,
Hammersmith, London W6 8JB

9 8 7 6 5 4 3 2 1

Anne Infante asserts the moral right to be identified
as the author of this work.

A catalogue record for this book is
available from the British Library

ISBN 0 00 232445 8

Photoset in Linotron Baskerville by
Rowland Phototypesetting Ltd
Bury St Edmunds, Suffolk
Printed and bound in Great Britain by
HarperCollins Book Manufacturing, Glasgow

IN APPRECIATION
This book is dedicated to the Ryan family who have
generously supported me from the start, who have launched
all my books with enthusiasm, and who have allowed me
to use their shop, The Mary Ryan Bookshop, as the
setting for *Death Launch*—as long as the chief bookseller
wasn't the murderer!
Thank you, Ryans and staff. It's a joy to have been
associated with you over the years.

ANNE INFANTE

CHAPTER 1

When my publisher, Alan Lewis, suggested Maddy Grey to launch my latest book I was less than thrilled, although I had to concede his point. Maddy was the perfect choice and the fact that I personally couldn't stand the woman was neither here nor there in Alan's eyes. She'd do a professional job, her name was synonymous with children and it was big enough to draw maximum media interest. What's more, it would fit in nicely with the proposed *Kids' World* deal I was still considering for Winifred Wombat.

'Riley's got the *Kids' World* franchise too, hasn't he? So it'll be good all round. Stuff your morals, Micky. Publishing is business.'

So Maddy was asked, she accepted, and the invitations were printed.

We had high hopes for *Winifred Joins the Chorus*. Ever since I'd created the ever hopeful wombat child with ballerina ambitions she'd been a hit. The idea of the little Aussie battler, following her dream against all the odds, caught children's imaginations. It was my way of letting them know that the greatest achievers in history were often the most unlikely candidates, but nothing can stop a determined dreamer who persists in the face of all opposition. In her tulle tu-tu she waddled and bounced gamely through several books, her eye on a star, the despair of Mrs Chumley-Smythe who owned the ballet school. Her juvenile readers adored her. I must admit, so did I. There's a lot of me in young Winifred.

I knew John Riley was even less enthusiastic than I was about asking Maddy, but he had his own reasons for keeping her sweet so he went along with Alan. He needed the

Kids' World products in his shop—they paid his rent each month.

It being Saturday morning, there wasn't a park to be had anywhere near Riley's, so I traded on my privileged status as successful local author and friend and squeezed the Capri into the few square inches of delivery space down the side of the shop. Who delivers on a Saturday, anyway? I left the keys in the ignition, just in case, and went around to the entrance.

Riley's, my favourite bookshop, fronts on to LaTrobe Terrace, which is the main road at the top of Paddington. A turn-of-the-century, white wooden affair, it clings to the steep hill in the suicidal fashion of Paddington buildings, its chin resting firmly on the narrow strip of ground at street level, its rear hanging dangerously on ungainly high stumps over a sharply sloping, multi-terraced garden. The shop awning reaches across the pavement, supported on white wooden pillars which rise from the kerb. It started life as a worker's cottage, like so many of the street front shops, and the owner maintained its original façade and atmosphere, thank God.

John Riley came from behind the counter, his good-natured face crinkling into a beaming smile, his hand outstretched in welcome.

'Micky! Great to see you, mate. Look, we're a bit busy . . .'

'We can manage for a while, John.' Barbara, John's wife, appeared at my side with an armful of books and tiptoed to give me a peck on the cheek. 'Hello, Micky.' She turned to John. 'I'm just topping up a few titles. It's mostly browsers now and Fi and I can manage. Take Micky down and have a cuppa and a chat.' She grimaced at me. 'John's been here since seven this morning. Hasn't even had breakfast.'

John hesitated and Barbara gave him a little push towards the stairs. 'Off with you both. Take him away, Micky.'

'She's the boss.' John laughed and led me to the back of the shop, threading his way through an assortment of book buffs. Riley's is as much a social tradition as a bookshop. You go there to browse, meet writers and true booklovers, catch up on the latest in the publishing world, pick up the monthly newsletter. John is a rare bird in the book trade these days, a man who eats, sleeps and lives books and recognizes and supports authors in the realization that, without them, there is no book industry, a point seemingly often missed by publishing companies.

I followed him to the internal staircase which led down a floor to the offices, amenities and storeroom. In one corner of the shop various children, only partially controlled by resigned parents, were ransacking the *Kids' World* shelves.

'That still going well for you?'

'Couldn't do without it, Micky.' He looked back at me as we descended, a worried crease between his brows. There seemed no reason for this, but John's a perpetual worrier. These days, working around the clock to keep the family firm alive, he's probably got good cause. What with the recession our former treasurer told the nation we had to have, plus the cost of wages, rent and taxes, small businesses are going to the wall in their hundreds.

Fiona, the Rileys' attractive daughter, passed us on the stairs and evened me up with a kiss on my other cheek.

'Mum just buzzed to say you were in. I'm going up to relieve Dad. Keep him down here for a while, Micky. He needs a break.'

We settled ourselves at the table on the small back verandah overlooking the garden and sipped our coffee. John sat back, running his hands through his greying hair. Below us, his son Don was setting up a trestle-table on the first terrace.

'We've got Robert Adams tonight, doing a chat about how he gets his ideas for his crime novels. He's sold the paperback rights to Pan and they've just released a set of three volumes. Looks good. They'll sell like hot cakes. Then we've got the kids' party tomorrow for Children's Book Week. Tony Ridgeway's speaking, and Bobby West. We're flat out with launches and promotions.'

'Will Maddy Grey be putting in an appearance?'

'No,' he said shortly. The worried frown was back. 'Her secretary called. Mrs Grey is—indisposed.'

'Hell!' I could feel my own forehead furrowing along with his. 'I hope she's sorted herself out by Monday week.'

John shrugged. 'Get Tony to talk to her. The launch'll be good publicity for her, which I gather she could use at the moment. Want me to ask him?'

'No, I'm on my way up to Channel 6 now to talk to Tony about the deal they're offering for my books. I'll have a word in his ear.'

'He's not so hot on Maddy at the moment. He called in yesterday for a drink and a chat and was very touchy on the subject. Rumour is she's been receiving offers from Channel 8 to drop Ridgeway and take *Kids' World* over to them.'

'Can she do that?'

'Oh yes, she owns the biggest chunk of the programme as well as the lion's share of the franchises. The woman may be a pain in the butt but she's smart.'

I watched Don arranging chairs for the patrons who didn't fancy the low wood-slat benches which were placed at intervals among the ferns and bushes in the garden and thought about *Kids' World*. It's the biggest children's TV programme in Australia, produced locally, received nationally. It's also sold to half a dozen countries overseas. Maddy Grey is its co-creator and hostess, Anthony Ridgeway the producer. It's been going for years. It saved Channel 6 when the station was in the red so deep it needed an urgent lifeline. Then along came Morgan Grey, TV producer and magnate, his young and beautiful wife Maddy, and *Kids' World*, which proceeded to knock all rival chil-

dren's shows out of the game. The spin-offs in books, audio
and video tapes, soft toys, games, children's clothing, tooth-
brushes, mugs—you name it, they produced it—made mil-
lions for Maddy, Morgan and Channel 6. It was Oz's
answer to the Muppets and Maddy shot to stardom which,
the scandal-mongers pointed out, was why she married a
man old enough to be her father in the first place.

After a dozen years of trying to keep her extra-marital
activities and increasingly heavy drinking out of the gossip
columns, Morgan finally went to his reward in that big TV
studio in the sky and Maddy took on a co-host, a likeable
young man in his early twenties, Bobby West. The scandal-
mongers whispered that he was Maddy's toy boy. I
didn't know and couldn't care less—except for feeling a
degree of pity for any male in Maddy Grey's clutches.

CHAPTER 2

I turned the car west and headed up Mount Coot-tha to
Channel 6. The mountain is still mostly unspoiled natural
bushland, some state forest, some privately owned and as
yet undeveloped. A single road, Sir Samuel Griffith Drive,
coils up to the summit, connecting the TV stations. At one
end, a lookout and restaurant perch precariously, offering
tourists spectacular views across the city to Moreton Bay.
It's a favourite spot for locals too. The Drive snakes across
the mountain top, unfolding an ever-changing panorama of
deep, heavily timbered valleys, sudden wide views across
farmland dotted with dams glistening silver in the distant
haze, and glimpses of Brisbane City far below. People come
up at night to enjoy the city lights. It's quite a show.

I turned into the Channel 6 entrance and convinced the
watchman at the gate that I hadn't come on nefarious business. He checked his visitor list and buzzed reception to let

them know I was on my way up, then pointed me towards the visitors' car park. I found a vacant space and walked up the steep hill, through carefully landscaped native gardens full of silver-leaved wattles and scarlet and golden banksia and bottlebrush. The bees were having a field day, hard at work from blossom to blossom, soaking up as much nectar and pollen as their fat little bodies could carry.

The meccano TV tower stretched into the sky above me as the path skirted around it up a series of timber steps to the main building. This was air-conditioned to cool, contrasting sharply with the heat of the day. The receptionist shifted her attention from a small TV screen on the wall opposite her desk and smiled brightly.

'Good morning, Mr Douglas. Please take a seat. Someone will be out to get you in a moment.'

Put like that it sounded like a threat, but I obediently took a seat in one of the lounge chairs that lined the walls. The sort I dislike—sit too far back and you'll never get out again. I perched on the edge and glanced around the room. The receptionist was a beautifully manicured fashion plate, more like a TV star than the official ones. The screen she'd been looking at was a black and white monitor, showing a view of the main gate, visitors' car park and path to the front door. She'd watched me all the way up. I surreptitiously checked to make sure I was tidy and smoothed my hair.

The stars of Channel 6 smiled down at me from the wall looking sultry, charming, witty, genial or professional, depending on their line of work. I idly scanned the portraits. Some I recognized: Maddy Grey; Rebecca Rowland, star of *Summer Days*, a local soapie; Frank Young, newsreader; Rhonda Ashley, anchorwoman of *Brisbane Update*, a current affairs programme. A large colour TV set was softly chattering away for the amusement of those waiting. It being Saturday morning, the programme was, of course, *Kids' World*, recorded through the week, put to air in the

prime time viewing spot for youngsters. Maddy Grey, surrounded by furry puppets and a vocal studio audience,
smiled serenely out to her young viewers across Australia,
taking the chaos in her stride, while an adoring tot pulled
at her dress. No wonder she drank. I watched her, catching
my breath slightly, as always. She certainly was beautiful
in an ethereal way, her white-blonde curls clustered around
her pale, fine-boned face in a style reminiscent of a Greek
statue, her eyes a wonderful, deep violet blue, her warm
mouth curved in a smile that had been the downfall of a
string of poor sods who had taken all that delicate beauty
and charm at face value and had reached out to caress a
kitten, only to find themselves entangled with a tiger.

A door opened and a young girl looked in. Her sulky
expression lightened when she saw me and she came across
quickly and gave me a hug.

'Hi, Micky! I was with Tony and thought I'd save Karen
the trip. Come on up.'

'Lead on, Angel. I've just been watching your mum do
her thing.'

The smile she'd donned for me left her face and she
scowled at the TV set and gave a snort of derision, but
made no comment until we were on the other side of the
door in the quiet, sunny corridor which led to the inner
sanctum.

'Turns it on like a tap!' my young escort said with a
bitterness that made my stomach churn. She strode briskly
past the stairs which led to the next floor, where the studios,
make-up and dressing-rooms were located, to a lobby taste-
fully decorated in smoke blue and apricot, the walls hung
with soft pastel prints. Stands of potted palms gave a lush,
tropical effect. Here she stopped and pushed a button on
the wall to summon the lift.

'How all those kids can believe all that lovey-dovey,
cooey rubbish beats me. The girls at school are always
going on about how lovely she is and how lucky I am and

how I look just like her.' She stabbed crossly at the button again to relieve her feelings, although the light was indicating an imminent arrival. 'I'd rather be bald, or dye my hair black and wear tinted contact lenses! I wish I'd been born dark like Dad instead of taking after *her*.'

The doors purred open and the plush designer lift invited us in. We accepted and were whisked up to the third-floor executive offices.

I watched Angela Grey, wishing for the umpteenth time that Morgan hadn't died and left her alone with Maddy. Her duties as a mother extended only to meeting physical needs. Angie had the best education, clothes, facilities and Nanny service that money could buy. She lived with Maddy in their luxury home in Paddington, and had her own gymnasium and indoor swimming pool which she never used, preferring to join her friends at the local youth club. She'd had ballet, piano, singing and drama lessons, which had turned her into a graceful, accomplished girl with all Maddy's charm and delicate blonde beauty. When she was a child she'd entered willingly into these pursuits, striving for excellence, trying desperately to win the approval of the mother she adored, taking Maddy's lack of interest as a sign that she was a failure in those beautiful eyes. Later, when I watched her come to the slow and painful recognition that her goddess had feet of clay and a heart of marble, I could cheerfully have strangled Maddy and never gone near her again. But Morgan had been a friend of mine and I felt the need to watch out for Angela and do whatever I could to counter Maddy's poison.

Morgan Grey and I went back a long way. We'd met at a festival of children's literature where we'd both been guest speakers. I was just starting my career—this was twenty years ago—he was a seasoned professional, writer, producer, already involved in *It's a Small World*, a children's radio programme, as well as producing a weekly TV drama. Despite the difference in our ages we developed a friendship that grew steadily deeper as the years passed. When Maddy came along she'd done her best to break up the relationship, jealous of anyone with a claim on Morgan's affection and suspicious of me in particular because I was fully aware, even as young and inexperienced as I was then, of the games Maddy played. Eventually she gave in and begrudgingly tolerated me as I tolerated her, for Morgan's sake.

When Angela was born I was on hand to babysit, read her endless stories, try out my new material on her, and be her uncle by adoption. After Morgan's death I felt no need to see Maddy on any regular basis but Angela and I remained as close as ever. We shared lunches and trips to the beach, she hauled me, protesting, on to wild rides at the Ekka (the Royal Brisbane Exhibition to you) and I encouraged her to try her hand at writing down the wonderful fantasies which sprang so easily to her mind.

Maddy didn't like our relationship but she'd learned not to interfere—I can out-stubborn her any day—so she smiled on us—but only on the surface. I knew that, but for Morgan's sake I liked to think I was somehow watching over his little girl.

Every day my dislike of what I was seeing grew. More and more, Maddy was taking out her frustrations on Angela in subtle ways, while still seeming everything a mother could be: because Angela was now becoming a serious liability in Maddy's eyes. She began to recognize her daughter as a rival and dreaded the inevitable comparisons that were made when the two were together. Maddy's fast lifestyle and bouts of drinking were making rapid inroads that, these days, took the girls in make-up longer to disguise. Maddy Grey was slowly coming apart.

The lift decanted us smoothly in a foyer full of muted colour and artistic flower arrangements. Angela opened a door and motioned me into Ridgeway's suite. A slim, dark girl rose from behind a grey steel desk and smiled a welcome. She was in her mid-twenties and wore a cream silk trouser suit and bright red scarf which set off her glossy dark curls. Karen Blair, Anthony Ridgeway's new, super-efficient secretary, much admired by Angela.

'She's so nice,' Angela had confided to me when Karen had arrived. Then, enviously, 'And she's *dark*. She's got dark brown hair and black eyes and a fabulous tan and she can wear *anything*!' She'd despairingly scanned her own fair skin, violet eyes and long, white-blonde plait in the mirror wall of the restaurant where I'd taken her for lunch. 'I'm so like *her*.'

'Cheer up,' I told her jokingly. 'You girls can always change colour.'

'She won't let me,' Angela said shortly. 'I tried to tell her it's embarrassing but she won't listen. Calls me "baby" in that soppy way and tells me I look just like she did at my age.'

I wondered why Maddy clung so stubbornly to Angela's fairness when it made her so angry. You'd think she'd be encouraging her look-alike daughter to change. No doubt a psychoanalyst would have an answer. Perhaps when she looked at Angie it gave her comfort to remember her own youthful beauty and helped her to briefly forget the pain of seeing herself rapidly ageing. I was vaguely aware that Maddy had never grown up and was narcissistic enough to simply not recognize the needs of others, like a child totally absorbed in her own wants, but I had no desire to make excuses for her and found it impossible to have compassion for her situation. She seemed enmeshed in a complicated web of resentment and revenge, but was too fearful to change the situation and lose the mirror of what she would still like herself to be. Her insecurities could keep a team of therapists in gourmet meals for years. Even her neuroses had neuroses.

At least Angie seemed to have found a sympathetic friend in the petite brunette who was thanking her for fetching me. I was introduced to Ridgeway's secretary, who smiled at me and immediately tapped on an inner door.

'Go right in, Mr Douglas. Mr Ridgeway is waiting for you.'

I looked at Angela. 'What are you going to do, Angel?'

'Can I come in with you, unless—' she eyed Karen hopefully—'is there anything I can do for you?'

'Not right now, Angela, unless you'd like to make coffee for Mr Ridgeway and Mr Douglas?'

'Oh, sure, great!' Angela beamed and disappeared, with a wave at me, through a matching door behind the secretary's desk.

I thought I heard Karen mutter 'poor kid', but the smooth, professional face was still politely smiling at me so I must have imagined it. I entered Ridgeway's office.

Tony Ridgeway couldn't survive in a muted pastel environment and he'd stamped his forceful personality on the office, which had been Morgan Grey's four years previously. There was a vivid abstract on one wall, a Lautrec poster opposite and a collection of model soldiers fighting Waterloo all over again on a table under the large picture window. A set of bookshelves was divided equally between Le Carré and Deighton novels and a collection of wooden African carvings, the latest in collectables.

Ridgeway shook my hand vigorously and drew up two comfortable chairs, motioning me to one. He didn't like doing business at Morgan's large oak desk, saying it put a barrier between him and his guest.

'Drink, Micky? Or Karen has coffee on the way, if you'd prefer.'

His voice was deep and attractive. An actor's voice.

'Coffee's fine, thanks, Tony. Angie's organizing it.'

'Right! We can get down to business.' He selected a manilla folder from his desk and settled himself opposite me.

'OK, Micky, I've been in touch with Alan Lewis and he's

ecstatic. He loves our approach with Winifred Wombat, the soft toys are going to be great—real winners. Just like the book illustrations—you know us, we keep to the originals. It'll be excellent for all of us and you know our terms are generous. That's always been my way. I give a lot to get a lot.' He eyed me speculatively. 'Now, Alan tells me the only snag is you. So I want you to be straight with me, Micky. What's the problem?'

I hesitated. I knew Ridgeway pretty well. When Morgan was executive producer Tony was his assistant, and that was going back fifteen years. He'd come up through the ranks, starting out as an actor, then moving into radio, first as an announcer, then on the production side. He'd joined *Kids' World* in 1976, a year after its debut. When Morgan died in 1987, Tony had stepped smoothly into his place. But the years of dealing with Maddy seemed to be taking their toll on him as well. His fair hair was showing a glint of silver, his light grey eyes looked tired. Perhaps he'd understand my reluctance better than most.

The door opened and Angela appeared doing her secretary act with a neatly set out tray. She dispensed coffee from a silver pot and sugared and creamed it to our specifications.

'Thanks, Angel.' I grinned at her. 'Come to me if you need a reference.'

'Can I stay or are you talking secrets?' She looked anxiously at Ridgeway.

'It's fine with me, Ange, if Micky doesn't mind.'

If I was going to come clean it couldn't be in front of Angela.

'Sorry, Angel, it's private for now.'

Her face fell. 'OK, that's fine. See you later.' The door closed behind her.

'What's she doing hanging around here?' I asked irritably, feeling her hurt at my rejection. 'Where's her mother?'

Ridgeway's handsome face darkened. 'Maddy tied one on with a vengeance last night. My fault, I'm sorry to say. Christ! You'd think by now I'd know better. She hit the kid about. Angie phoned me and I picked her up and took her home to stay with Becky and me. I couldn't leave her with that bitch.'

I felt sick. 'What was it about?'

'I put my foot in it properly, Micky. There's a new slot opening in *Kids' World.* Just a minor part—five minutes out of the hour. We were thinking of using a young girl and I suggested we try Angie. Maddy chucked a bloody mental. Shit! Why did she go to all that trouble to train the kid? Acting, singing, dancing? Angie could do very well in TV given half a chance and she wants to try. I told Maddy, just a tiny part, they wouldn't be on screen together, we could put Ange in a wig if Maddy wanted—well, Micky, I don't have to tell you what the problem is there! But she did her block! Accused me of all sorts, from wanting her dead to God knows what, and told Angie she was an ungrateful little tart, and worse, and she'd never allow her to appear as long as she had any say in it. Well, she's the mother. It's her signature we'd need on the contract. Oh Christ!' He shook his head. 'Yeah, I know, Micky. Don't think I haven't told myself I'm all kinds of a fool, but Angie's so keen, she's been throwing out feelers all year to be given a test. It seemed the perfect opportunity. We could even change her name. Who'd know she was Maddy's kid?'

I knew it wouldn't matter. All Maddy's fears had suddenly fused into reality and she'd lost all sense of proportion.

'Anyway, Maddy's at home sleeping it off, I hope, so I brought Ange in with me. Bobby West's in the studio. She likes to watch his segments being filmed. We're trying to get ahead so we can concentrate on Maddy's stuff when she's—when she's better,' he finished resignedly.

I knew it wasn't any use telling Ridgeway what a

complete prat he'd been. He knew it already. And it made it easier to discuss my problem with him. He was looking the question at me. I took a deep breath and leaned forward in my chair.

CHAPTER 3

Tony Ridgeway lit a cigarette and sat back, watching the smoke curl and drift.

'So that's it?' he said at last and tapped a quiet percussion on the cigarette packet. 'Not very businesslike, Micky.'

'So, sue me,' I told him and added hastily, 'Only joking, Tony.'

His pained expression lightened and he gave me a tired smile. 'You know me, Micky, I don't come the heavy. Nothing that can't be talked out, I reckon. There's always a way for everyone to win; but—' he dropped the packet on to the low table between us—'you can't be serious, mate. I know Maddy can be a pain, but you've got everything to gain here.'

'I know,' I agreed, 'but I just don't fancy the idea of selling Maddy Grey the rights to Winifred Wombat, which is what it amounts to. It's true, I don't like the woman and I certainly don't trust her, but it's more than that. I've a bad feeling about this whole thing and that's something I can't rationalize and it makes me very reluctant to agree to the deal.'

'Talk to Maddy,' he urged. 'You've known her a long time, Micky. Sit down with her and work it out.'

'In her present state?' I asked ironically.

'She'll be right as rain in a day or two, you know that. Give her a bell and get together. You'd be a damn fool to let personal feelings get in the way of this.'

I smiled slightly. 'The truth is, Tony, I don't particularly need this deal but I get the impression that Maddy does. I don't see myself enriching her coffers and I don't want her to get her hands on Winifred.'

'Christ, Micky!' He slapped his hand on the arm of his chair in exasperation. 'And you tell me she's childish!' Then he stopped, his mouth tightly shut and looked at me thoughtfully. After a moment he leaned forward confidingly.

'OK, Micky, I know you and your feelings and I'm not going to beat my head against a brick wall. I'm going to say something that's completely confidential. Not to go beyond this room, right?'

'Right,' I assured him, wondering what was coming.

'You don't want to let Maddy get hold of your little wombat, but just supposing it wasn't Maddy? That she wasn't the host of *Kids' World*? How'd you feel about it then?'

I was silent. It looked as if John Riley's rumour might just be true.

'You mean, if Maddy went to 8?'

He nodded slowly. 'I know there's been gossip. Hell, it's the name of the game. But it's a fact Maddy's been seeing Gaby Mentos. She hasn't said anything to me, but she's sure as hell thrown out enough hints. Holding it over me to get me to agree to her demands or she'll take the show. I can tell you, on the QT, that she can't actually do that, but Micky—' he dropped his voice—'between you and me, it wouldn't break my heart if Maddy left *Kids' World*. Bobby West's going pretty well—won the viewers' choice for most popular newcomer at the Logies in his first year. He could host the show standing on his head. And I'd bring Angie in. They'd be magic together. Now, in those circumstances, what would you say?'

'I'd wait and see.' I grinned suddenly. '*Kids' World* is Maddy's baby and I can't see her leaving it in the hands of Bobby West and Angela.'

'I don't agree.' He still leaned forward, speaking in that confidential tone. 'Gabrielle Mentos is very keen to have her and Maddy's just angry enough to give 6 the push, even if it meant leaving *Kids' World* here and starting over. You think about it, Micky.'

'I'll do that,' I promised. 'Look, there's another thing, Tony. A bit of a cheek to ask you after I've as good as turned you down, but we're concerned about the launch. Could you keep an eye on Maddy, make sure she's OK on the night?'

'She'll do it, Micky. She owes you, mate. I'll see to it. She needs some good publicity right now. I'll be coming along too, showing the flag, and we'll bring Bobby. Becky'll be in it, she'll draw the media.' Becky Ridgeway, Tony's wife, was the lovely Rebecca Rowland, soap star. 'We'll get Channel 6 behind Winifred one hundred per cent and maybe you'll see what a mistake it'd be not to let us use her in the show.'

I'll give it to Ridgeway, he's an eternal optimist. I got up to take my leave and he grinned at me. 'I'll keep on you, you know. Constant drops of water wear away stone in the end. Now I'm due downstairs. We've got a tight schedule on *Kids' World* and, with Maddy out to it for God knows how long, we're pre-taping as much of Bobby as we can so we can get ahead. But Maddy'll have to pull herself together soon.'

There was a discreet tap on the door and Karen entered. 'Excuse me, Mr Ridgeway, you said to remind you of the time.'

'Yeah, thanks, love. I'm on my way. Come down with me, Micky, and watch young West go through his paces. He'd do a great job with Winifred.'

I nodded and watched Karen watching Ridgeway. A bad case of hero worship there, if I wasn't mistaken. Tony always could pull the birds. In the early days he'd been a big, blond surfer type with never less than three girls on a string. Maddy had made a play for him from the outset but he was always way too smart to mess with the boss's wife.

We rode the lift to the first floor and walked down more long, quiet corridor, past a sitting-room, a kitchenette where someone was making toast and an appetizing smell of fresh-brewed coffee hung in the air, past the open door of the make-up room with its mingled scents of hairspray, powder and cosmetics, and around the corner to the studios. The far door had a red light glowing above it and a large notice warning people not to enter when the red light was on. Ignoring both, Ridgeway pushed the heavy soundproofed door and went in, beckoning me to do the same. I shrugged and followed him into the studio.

The floor was shrouded in shadows. To the left, half a dozen metal chairs were pushed against the wall and I trod softly over to them, stepping over heavy cables, and took a seat. Angela was there, absorbed, her chin in her hands, watching the brightly lit dais in the centre of the room which was the focus of attention. Three large cameras on dollys wheeled slowly back and forth, their operators receiving silent instructions through headphones from Wes Martin, the director. In a corner, two girls in jeans and sloppy joes emblazoned with the *Kids' World* logo quietly sorted through a mountain of envelopes on the floor, peering at each one before either discarding it or dropping it into a large perspex barrel mounted on a frame so it could be easily spun around. Angela gave me a brief smile and I pointed to the barrel, my eyebrows asking a silent question.

'Competition,' she hissed, 'answers on the back of an envelope. Bobby'll draw out the winner later.'

Overhead, a battery of lights hung in the gloom on low scaffolding; at the rear of the stage area tall stands of wooden benches rose towards them for the days when the show was filmed before a live audience.

In the glare of lights in the centre of the room, Bobby West, wearing identical gear to the barrel attendants, was singing a bright little song with appropriate actions. Behind him, a group of furry puppets joined enthusiastically in the chorus, manipulated by three silent, black-garbed figures, barely discernible. I didn't realize they were miming to a tape until Bobby stopped and the music went on.

The cameras halted, auto cues began to roll back to a pick-up point, Bobby smiled a gentle apology and looked across to a small knot of men who'd been joined earlier by Ridgeway.

'Sorry, Wes, I lost it. Can we run it from the top again?'

A small man with thinning ginger hair, a harried expression and half glasses perched on his nose hurried up to the dais to consult with the co-star. A make-up girl materialized from the shadows and began to flick Bobby's face over with a powder brush and comb his hair. 'You're getting shiny,' she reproved him. He seemed almost unaware of her attentions and continued in conversation with the director who, after a brief burst of arm waving and rapid nodding, peered through the lights to the envelope sorters.

'We'll do the barrel next,' he warned them. The make-up girl quietly slipped across to give the others a hand, the camera men turned their attention back to the action, the music rolled again, Bobby West strutted his stuff, the onlookers went back to their whispered conversation. Beside me, Angela hummed the tune under her breath and unconsciously mimed West's movements.

With an appalling crash, the studio door flew open and an angry voice was raised.

'I'll go where I bloody well please. This is *my* studio, *my* show. Keep *off* me, you bitch!'

We all froze as Maddy Grey half fell into the room, locked in the arms of Karen Blair.

CHAPTER 4

Karen said breathlessly, 'I'm sorry, Mr Ridgeway, I couldn't stop her.' She looked frightened. Maddy advanced on the producer, an expression of such fury on her face that Tony took an involuntary step backwards. One of the barrel girls gave a faint shriek and stuffed her fist against her mouth. I became aware of Angela gripping my arm, watching her mother with a sort of fascinated horror.

'You bastard!' The usually pale, delicate face was flushed, the white-gold hair dishevelled. 'You're trying to take over my show, you and your precious protégé. I know what you want. You want me to go over to Gaby and you think you'll put that boot-licking little toad in my place. Well, let me tell you something, Tony Ridgeway.' She thrust her angry face up at his and I could see tiny drops of spittle on his cheek, glinting in the spill of fierce light. 'You think you're so clever, you've got it all worked out. Well, think again, my friend.' Her voice dripped with venom. '*I* found Bobby West and he's contracted to me and *Kids' World*. You can throw me out but you won't get the show. You look at my contract again. Morgan and I owned *Kids' World* and it's mine now, not the channel's. If I go, I take the show with me. And I'll do it, too. Take it to Channel 8, and then where will you be, Mr Clever Ridgeway?'

Tony didn't turn a hair, just stood looking down at her, seeming unmoved after that one backward step. His voice was quiet, contrasting with her rage, but it carried around the studio.

'I don't think you'll do that, Maddy. I've had the solicitors looking over all the contracts. You're perilously close to losing yours, and your control of *Kids' World*. You have a clause that guarantees a certain standard and regularity of work. We're not seeing much of that lately.' He took her arm and she stared up at him, her mouth working but with no sound coming. 'Now, Maddy, you're interrupting the show and embarrassing all of us. You don't want to put Angela through this, do you?'

She looked around wildly. 'Angela? Baby? Where are you? Look what they're doing to poor Maddy, baby. Don't let them do this, darling.'

Angela stiffened. 'Oh hell!' she said in despair. 'I wish she . . .' Then she released her grip on my arm and stepped forward calmly.

'I'm here, Mum.' She went over to Maddy and put her arms around her. Maddy seemed to shrink against her and I realized with a shock that Angela was playing the mother now. 'Come on, Mum, you'd better come home.'

'Baby.' Maddy peered at her. 'They're all against me, all of them. Gaby's the only one I can trust. Tony and Bobby and Jessica and that awful Fry woman and now that little tart in Tony's office—they all hate me, they all wish me dead, baby.'

Angela's voice was soothing. 'No they don't, Mum. They just want you to get better and come back to the show. They need you, they all need you. You ARE *Kids' World*. They know that.'

Maddy reared back suspiciously. 'Now I remember. You want me out, too. You want to take over the show. You're with them. My own daughter!'

'No, Mum, you're wrong. I don't want that. You're terrific in the show, really. All the kids love you. I couldn't do it. You're the star.'

'Bobby!' Maddy hissed. 'He's doing the show by himself. Why else is he here? He's going behind my back. I found him, I put him where he is, he belongs to me. Get him off the stage!'

'He's just doing his bits to get ahead until you're back.' Angela was stroking her mother's hair. 'No one's trying to hurt you, Mum. Come on, we'll get Karen to call a taxi and I'll take you home. On Monday you'll be back and it'll be OK. The show must go on, you've always told me that.'

Maddy gave a wavering smile. 'Yes, yes, the show must go on. And I *am* the show, you said so.'

'It's true, Mum.' Angela signalled Karen, who slipped away. Tony put out a hand but Angela shook her head and led her mother out. The door closed quietly behind them and Tony wiped his face with a handkerchief.

For a moment nobody moved and then a little tremor ran around the room and Wes Martin clapped his hands.

'All right, pick it up, people. Girls, get that barrel ready. We've wasted enough time.'

Tony came over to me. 'Christ, Micky, I'm sorry! They had instructions not to let her in if she came around. It's happened before.'

I looked at him squarely. 'Maddy seemed pretty sure that she owns *Kids' World* and you can't do anything about it.'

'Don't you believe it.' He dropped his voice in obedience to a signal to the room. 'She's violated her contract a dozen times. We'll keep the show all right. Now, settle down and get a load of Bobby.'

But I'd had enough of *Kids' World* for one day. I made my excuses and left to the tune of Bobby West's 'I Can March Like A Soldier'.

I drove home thinking about the scene I'd just witnessed, wondering if Maddy would carry out her threat and take *Kids' World* to Channel 8 and if Tony had the power to stop her through the reliability clause. I considered that clause with approval. Maddy would never have signed such a condition off her own bat.

You cunning old devil! I told Morgan Grey silently. You knew what she was like when you married her, you fox. That must have been your doing.

It gave me comfort to realize that, although Morgan had been genuinely in love with his capricious wife, he hadn't been blind to her character. He was always the business man.

'Good on you, mate,' I said aloud.

Of course, it would probably end up a flash in the pan as usual. Maddy was in the habit of making almighty scenes, offending even her closest friends and being generally obnoxious for days when her insecurities and the drink overwhelmed her. Then she'd revert magically to a sweet-tempered, charming creature and woo her court back with apologies and specially selected little gifts. Sometimes I wondered if the whole performance was deliberately staged for effect. You couldn't believe a word the woman said.

I thought about Angela, taking charge of the situation, soothing her angry mother, mature beyond her years. You'd have to grow up fast around Maddy. There wouldn't be much that life could surprise you with after her. I was now unhappily aware of another possible reason for Maddy's fear of her daughter. Being seen around with Bobby West made Maddy look good, gave her a young image, boosted her ego. I'd seen the way Angela had watched him and the smile he'd flashed at her during the break in filming. Also, when Angela had gone to her mother, West had made a movement as if to join her, but the girl, seemingly deeply attuned to him, had suddenly looked around and signalled him to stay out of it. He'd remained on the dais, the harsh spot lights betraying his anxiety. I grimaced. If Maddy had the slightest suspicion of that situation she'd give Angela all kinds of hell.

I parked outside 18 Princess Road, under the huge Moreton Bay fig which spends its life quietly devouring the concrete footpath and dropping its sticky fruit on to anything it can reach, and ran up the steps to the red-brick, Victorian house, now divided into six flats. I live at the top, up two flights of stairs. My flatmate was waiting for me outside

No. 5, having let herself into the house through the cat flap in the back screen door. I'd left her doing T'ai-chi under the mango tree with fellow tenant Al Wang. She rose gracefully, yawned widely and stood, dog-like, with her nose against the door.

I let us both in and rewarded her patience with a saucer of tinned milk—her addiction. She's named for it—Carnation Belle Douglas, aristocratic Abyssinian, CF, DM (Clawer of Furniture, Destroyer of Manuscripts). She approached this offering with the disdain proper to one of her ancient and regal lineage, then forgot herself and, purring with ecstasy, slopped it all over her chin.

I settled down with the paper and looked for Jessica Savage's weekly column, The Savage Report. Something had triggered Maddy's outburst. Usually, after the sort of scene with Angela the previous night that Tony had described, Maddy would sleep it off and awake in the morning, all sweetness and light. So something had put her back on the boil. In her confused accusations I'd caught Jessica's name. Maddy had all the papers delivered for her secretary to clip any publicity items, *Kids' World* reviews or references to her goings-on in the gossip columns.

I found the page and grinned. It was there all right, with an unflattering photograph taken at some night club, catching the star at an awkward angle with her mouth open. She looked half cut but probably wasn't. So far, Maddy had kept her binges at home. She drank very little in public, keeping her wits about her to protect her *Kids' World* image.

Jessica also knew about Gabrielle Mentos's offer and, in her usual unrelenting fashion, hinted that Gaby might regret the impulse to filch Maddy from Channel 6 and that at least one of the station's producers might be rather relieved to see her go.

'That little affair was over as soon as it began,' Jessica had written, 'and no doubt said producer counts his blessings daily. Our would-be siren is not always so easy to shake off once her victims wake up to all her tricks and it takes desperate measures to unlock her platinum shackles once the poor mutts are back in their right senses. Gentlemen, beware! Perhaps a certain children's hostess should carry a public health warning clearly visible somewhere on her deceptive packaging. I suspect a certain newsreader would agree with me.'

I wondered vaguely who Jessica was hinting about. Certainly there'd been several producers over the years who fitted the bill, not as loyal to Morgan as Tony Ridgeway, and a couple were still with the channel—and at least two newsreaders. Bradley Wilson who hosted *Good Morning*, an hour of news and interviews, had been seen out with Maddy, as had Russell Scott, the late night newsreader.

Of course, in Maddy's better moods, she'd laugh off Jessica's digs. That was an old rivalry. Back in the early 'seventies, Jessica Savage and Morgan Grey had been a very hot item and were living together when the beautiful young Madeline Porter appeared on the scene, having won a bit part in a film Morgan was producing. She was just eighteen and Morgan was forty and divorced with a son Maddy's age. The producer was completely infatuated. Within a month Jessica was out and Maddy had moved in with Morgan. The following year they were married. Maddy was fully aware of the blow she'd dealt the older woman and shrewd enough to realize the cause of Jessica's vitriolic attacks. She'd once told me that she was flattered rather than offended, because she'd won where Jessica had failed and the whole world knew it and would put such remarks down to spite. But these days Jessica was getting more and more under Maddy's rapidly thinning skin.

The phone rang and a soft, breathless voice said, 'Micky? Micky Douglas? Guess who this is?' and giggled slightly.

'Gillian,' I said at once, 'Gillian Fry.'

She gave a delighted little laugh. 'I didn't think you'd remember—such a long time.'

'Not so long,' I protested jovially. 'I couldn't forget you, Gillian.' Damn, I thought, why do I always sound like the original patronizing bastard around Gillian? I forced myself back to normality. 'What are you doing these days?'

'Oh, writing, this and that, you know,' she said vaguely. 'I'm coming to your launch. I was in Riley's earlier and saw the flyer on the counter. Another of little Winifred's adventures. Good for you.'

'Are you publishing anything at the moment?'

'Well, not exactly—er—look, Micky,' she floundered, then said in a rush, 'I'd really like to talk. John Riley suggested I call you. Could we have lunch? I'm just down the road from Riley's now. We could meet at Henri's if you like.' Then she stopped and gave a little gasp. 'You'll probably think I'm awful, ringing you up and asking you out.' She ended abruptly with a nervous, high-pitched laugh.

I did a quick think. Gillian's a strange mixture. She lives on her nerves and her breathy, hesitant manner and self-deprecating giggles are par for the course. But there was something else in her soft voice, a note of anxiety different from the norm. I thought, if John Riley suggested we get together, then he must know something.

'I'd love to, Gilly,' I assured her. 'Give me ten minutes.'

Henri's was in one of the new complexes at the city end of Paddington. Once a lower-class area, full of workers' cottages, the old suburb was discovered by the yuppies who began to restore the houses to their former charm. They were followed by developers who, in their own blinkered fashion, with eyes firmly fixed on dollars instead of the historical atmosphere, began to demolish blocks of original buildings and create curving structures of steel and glass which go under the general heading of plazas and where anyone with visions of owning his or her own little shop is charged astronomical rents. One trendy place after another opens with a fanfare and closes within the year, to be refitted for the next hopeful. Henri Piccard was one of the rare stayers at the West Plaza, except lately even his custom was falling off as hard times closed down his neighbours. However, he still claimed you couldn't go wrong with food. 'Everyone has to eat, Micky,' and he specialized in healthy smorgasbord lunches at low prices and a range of delectable Continental pastries that slide down easily with a cup of his famous coffee, a special blend known only to himself. You can buy a bag, freshly ground, and try to figure out for yourself what mix he uses. He certainly won't tell you. His décor was simple; bare wooden tables, shining copper implements, farmhouse kitchen chintz.

Henri's was at the back of the plaza, between Chocs and The Perfect Gift, which used to be Adam's Gear for Men. The air was scented with pot-pourri from barrels just inside the door of The Perfect Gift, presumably to lure the customers into the interior crammed with every conceivable knick-knack. Elegant porcelain figurines jostled for space with gift baskets of organic soaps and exotic bath oil pearls, tiny crystal birds sparkled on a revolving tray, throwing rainbow lights on to brass mobiles suspended just above head height. If I ever went in there I'd probably smash something in the clutter of breakables. I passed on to Henri's.

Gillian had reserved a front table for two by the glass café front and was scanning the passers-by with a little worried frown. It was at least two years since I'd seen her but she hadn't changed. Tall and thin, she seemed to droop into herself like a wilting dahlia, a shock of pale brown hair cut almost into an Afro heightening the illusion. She stood up awkwardly when she saw me and held out her hand quickly.

'How lovely—you look just the same—nice to see you, Micky. You must be wondering what on earth . . .'

I shook her thin hand which always felt as though it would splinter under the slightest pressure.

'Hello, Gilly. I'm glad to see you.'

'Oh,' she said, slightly flustered, 'yes, yes, well, I hoped you wouldn't mind.'

'Not a bit.' I smiled at her. 'Let's get our lunch and then we can settle down and you can tell me all about it.' Oh God, I thought, I'm doing it again.

We chose our meal from the servery at the counter which was crowded with cold cuts, cheeses, quiches and bowls of fresh salad. Henri promised to bring a cheese platter over to our table and a carafe of his house white and we settled down to eat.

Gillian chattered aimlessly about various mundane topics, pausing every now and then to peer at me nervously and giggle. I answered her cheerfully and poured her a second glass of wine before interrupting the inconsequential flow.

'Gilly, it really is nice to see you, but I got the feeling there was something bothering you. Do you want to tell me what's wrong?'

She made a choking sound and grabbed at her knife which had slipped from her fingers. It fell with a crash on to her plate and she wiped it nervously with her napkin. When she looked up again her soft brown eyes were filled with tears.

'I'm in awful trouble,' she whispered. 'I—I haven't any right to ask you, but—but John thought—Micky, please help me.'

CHAPTER 5

Gillian rummaged helplessly in her large brown leather handbag and finally dragged out a handkerchief. She dabbed at her eyes and then began to twist the thin square of material between her restless fingers.

'It's Fantail,' she said huskily. 'They—they won't

publish my latest book. They said—it's too—too—violent and, yes, and sex—they said too much sex; not realistic, they said and—and offensive. It's *not*, Micky. No more than the others.'

I raised my eyebrows. She pounced on my expression like a terrier. 'I was surprised, too. I said it's not as much as *Terror Canyon* or *Last Train* and, well, you know, it's just the way they are, teenagers. This one is good. It's called *City Tribe* and it's about street kids. My agent thinks it's the best I've done.'

I looked at Gillian. She's awkward, shy and self-effacing. She dresses almost dowdily in out of date prints with calf-length skirts and bows. She hardly speaks above a whisper and, in spite of her height, is frequently overlooked in a crowd, even by her friends. She has a knack of disappearing into corners and peering nervously out at the world. And she writes brilliant, hard-hitting, uncompromising novels for teenagers which strike such a chord of recognition in her readers that she regularly tops the best-seller lists. Before I met her I'd read *Last Train*. It was a frank, totally honest, even frightening account of the despair of the teenage years. It made me recall with deep discomfort the way it had been for me and I applauded any author who could expose so unerringly the pain and uncertainty of youth. I'd imagined a young, hard, rebellious person and was totally unprepared for the shock of Gillian Fry. I couldn't for the life of me see from what part of her she created her disturbing stories. Her publishers, Fantail Press, had made a fortune out of her.

'But your books are immensely popular,' I protested. 'They can't be serious! Surely they'd simply request a rewrite of whatever parts they're objecting to.'

She shook her head and dabbed at her face with the mangled hanky. 'They won't consider it. I finally went to Derek Jones, the Managing Director, you know, and asked him right out.'

I couldn't imagine Gillian confronting anyone in
authority and asking him right out. I blinked at her, catching an almost fierce expression on her timid face.

'And?'

'He told me.' She nodded quickly several times. 'Yes, he
told me. He was really sorry but he said there wasn't anything he could do about it. If they publish *City Tribe* they'll
face a lawsuit and—and—' tears started to roll down her
thin cheeks—'it's all my fault. It was something I did.
Micky, please, please, will you talk to her, ask her to change
her mind? John Riley says you're a friend of hers.'

'Whoa!' I stopped her. 'You've lost me, Gilly. Who's a
friend of mine?'

Her soft brown eyes opened in surprise. 'Madeline Grey,
of course.'

It's not easy to follow Gillian at the best of times. My
mouth dropped as I latched on to the only recognizable
thing she'd said.

'John Riley told you I'm a *friend* of Madeline Grey?'

'Well, he said you knew her. She's launching your book,
after all.'

'Through no fault of my own,' I said tartly. 'What on
earth has Maddy Grey got to do with your book not being
published?'

'Oh, didn't I say? How silly of me. I'll forget my own
name next.' She gave me a watery smile. 'Well, when *Terror
Canyon* was published, instead of the usual launch, Fantail
held a competition for the readers and the winners were
invited to a special party with a couple of pop stars and,
well, me, to meet them. And one of the children, one of
the winners, was a lovely girl who looked very sad about
something and I started talking to her. It always helps, you
know, to be able to tell someone what's wrong, especially
if they just listen and don't bother you with advice. Well—'
she drew a breath and suddenly took up where she'd left
off—'yes, well, this poor thing was having trouble with an

awful mother who drank and hit her and she was talking about running away from home and wondered how she'd manage. We started to talk about street kids and she said there was a sort of code, a belonging, like they were all part of a tribe.' She stopped and was silent for a while, remembering. 'Poor child, she was only twelve. She had a bruise on her cheek, lovely fair skin, Scandinavian type, and the whitest blonde hair. I thought she'd been at the peroxide bottle but she said no, it was natural. Her name was Angela.'

The muscles in my stomach were a tight knot. I remembered Angela's excitement at the prospect of meeting her favourite author as clearly as I remembered the ugly bruise on her cheek.

'How did you get that, Angel?' I'd touched it gently, worried.

'It's all right.' She'd jerked her head away, flushing slightly. 'I fell down at gym. Clumsy.' But Angela was never clumsy. I'd assumed the floor must have been slippery or something.

I saw Gillian watching me with consternation. 'Why do you look like that, Micky? What's wrong?'

'Nothing.' I brought my attention back with an effort to her unhappy face. 'Go on, Gilly.'

'Well, afterwards, she said she felt better for talking to me and she'd work it out somehow. And her story stuck in my mind. I began to talk to children I saw in the city. I met some of the street kids and I used the name "City Tribe", remembering that sad child at the party. And— and I used her as well. I put her in the book. She was the main character. I didn't know who she was. You know, don't you? You must know her.'

'Yes,' I said gently, 'I know Angela Grey.'

Gillian twisted her handkerchief some more and seemed to wilt even further. 'Well—well, I was doing an interview and the journalist asked about my next project and I told her about the girl at the party and that I'd used her in the book. It was—it was Jessica Savage. She doesn't normally do that sort of interview but the journalist who was supposed to see me was sick and Jessica said she'd fill in for her. My bad luck. She—she—she *knew*, Micky, she recognized Angela Grey from my description and told me who it had been. Then she went behind my back and told Madeline Grey that I'd used her daughter in my book and Madeline would be exposed for what she was. She couldn't avoid twisting the knife, of course. I might have known!'

From the corner of my eye I could see Henri approaching with the cheese platter and our coffee. I raised a warning finger at Gillian. Henri shot a discreet look at her and rapidly cleared the plates.

'Is everything all right?' he asked me quietly.

'Yes, thanks, Henri. We won't bother about sweets—unless?'

Gillian shook her head. 'I couldn't. I'll have some cheese and crackers, though.'

Henri gave me a conspiratorial look of sympathy for a fellow man in a difficult situation and retreated.

'I take it Maddy has threatened to sue Fantail if they publish?' Gillian gave a little gasp and nodded. 'But surely you could get another publisher, Gilly. You're a big name.'

'It wouldn't matter. I had a letter from her secretary, Tracey Whitehead. Mrs Grey says she'll sue anyone who touches my books and make it so hot for them they'll regret it.' She looked pleadingly at me. 'You know what a tight market it is, Micky. I'd be branded too difficult to handle. I couldn't bear it. John Riley says she'll listen to you, that you know her and she's going to have Winifred Wombat on *Kids' World*.'

I shrugged helplessly. 'No one can reason with Maddy when she goes off her rocker like that. She's never heard of backing down and she doesn't accept compromise. Couldn't you shelve the book for now and do another one?'

Gillian's face flushed. She looked angry and her voice was even more breathless.

'Why should I? It's the best thing I've ever done. Those young people deserve to have their story told. If you can't help me, I'll speak to her myself. I—I'll find a way. I won't give up *City Tribe*.'

'Change the main character, then. Give her a different name and colouring, if that's the problem.'

Gillian's face closed, as near to stubborn as I'd ever seen her.

I shook my head. 'Well, I'll do my best, Gilly, but I think you'll have to alter the book in the end.'

She dropped her mulish expression and her eyes filled again. 'It wouldn't do any good.' She gave me a frightened look. 'She rang me. She'd been drinking. She—she swore at me!' Gilly looked shocked at the memory as if she was innocent of the language in her books. 'She said she—she'd get me, that I'd corrupted her daughter, that she wouldn't rest until I was finished. She said she'd make sure I'd never be published again. Micky—' she swallowed, her face livid. 'What on earth am I going to do?'

CHAPTER 6

Certain women of my acquaintance tell me I'm a chauvinist. By this they mean that I'm a sucker for any woman who looks at me with a helpless expression and tells me a sob story.

'You just have to be in like Galahad,' they say with disgust. 'You think the almighty male can solve all a girl's problems. It's an insult to women to assume they aren't just as capable as you are.'

If I dare to open my mere male mouth to protest, it's the worse for me.

'You're an endangered species,' they rage, 'the last of a dying breed. What makes you think you have to come riding to the rescue.'

My sister Susan, who lives in Sydney with her husband, Gerard, and my niece and nephew, was the first to tell me this, followed by Laney, my very liberated Great-Aunt Melanie Carter-Jones (don't tell her I let on she was my great-aunt. She may be old in years but she hasn't realized it yet). Monica Wainwright, owner, caretaker and den-mother of 18 Princess Road, added her mite two days after I moved in after a broken marriage, and Annie Mason, a fellow—no—person tenant (sorry, ladies, it slipped out) I once—er—knew, took up the chorus.

Girls, what can I say? I know women are just as capable as men. I know they are responsible, equal—even better at many things, tougher when it comes to the sight of blood and safer drivers, and I have never been guilty of telling any woman that it's just a phase she's going through, so I hope that if God does turn out to be female after all, She chalks that one up to me; only I wish the said ladies would get together and agree the rules, because there was Gillian Fry looking at me with tears in her eyes and asking for my help, so she obviously didn't know certain women of my acquaintance. And of course, being only a man and already confused about the weaker sex suddenly turning into the stronger sex almost overnight, I felt that old, outdated stirring in my breast. That is my defence, ladies of the jury, so please be lenient.

'I think you're over-estimating Maddy,' I said sensibly. 'She may threaten but she'd never be able to carry it out. How could she prevent your books being published, after all? You change *City Tribe* and she won't have a leg to stand on.'

'You don't know.' Gilly looked at me earnestly. 'She's powerful and she can make a lot of trouble. Tell stories about me, carry out a campaign—she said she'd do it. And she knows things about people. She said she had the dirt on all sorts of people in the publishing world and she had a lot of influence. No one wants that sort of trouble, especially as it's such a tight market. Anyway, she said she'd use her position to advise people against supporting certain publishers. They'd weigh up the odds against taking my books and I'd lose. She made that very clear.'

Maddy sounding off again, but she'd certainly intimidated Gillian sufficiently. I saw the desperation in her eyes. She believed Maddy all right. I sighed. I'd have to see what I could do to help, but I dreaded the inevitable confrontation.

As it happened, I didn't have to call Maddy. Later that afternoon she rang me.

'Micky,' she cooed into the phone, 'Angela tells me you were in the studio this morning. What a shame I missed you. And you came about Winifred Wombat, too.'

'I saw you,' I said drily.

'Oh dear, I'm afraid I was behaving very badly. I haven't been well lately and I had the most awful headache but Angela's been wonderful and I'm much better now. She's a treasure. I don't know what I'd do without my Angel.'

I thought of a dozen things to say but couldn't get any of them out. Maddy said, 'Hello, hello, are you still there Micky?'

'I'm here.'

'I thought we'd been cut off. Now, I want to talk to you. We're such old friends I know we can sort something out. Tony came over earlier and told me some ridiculous thing about you not wanting us to use Winifred. I expect he's got it all wrong, as usual.'

'No,' I told her, 'he hasn't got it wrong.'

'Oh! Now, Micky, that's just plain silly. We're all really looking forward to using her. It'll make you a fortune. Morgan would have been so delighted.' She paused but I didn't bite. 'Look, how would it be if Bobby read the stories?

You saw him today, didn't you? He's wonderful, absolutely right for Winifred. I adore Bobby's work and I'm behind him one hundred per cent of the time, you know.'

I thought of the way Brutus had been one hundred per cent behind Cæsar, but said, 'You didn't seem very happy with him earlier.'

She gave her low, husky laugh. 'Oh, now, don't be awful to me. You know I sometimes get a bit upset and say things I don't really mean. Bobby's tops in my book. Why don't you come over for dinner and we'll discuss it.'

'There *is* something I want to talk about.' I decided to strike while the iron was hot. Maddy seemed to be back in one of her good moods.

'Darling, anything I can do for you, just tell me.'

'I had lunch with Gillian Fry today.' There was a silence at the other end and I tried to sense if she was simply waiting for me to continue or was going off the rails again. I blundered on. 'She's a bit upset. Probably all a misunderstanding. She thinks you're going to sue her publishers if they accept her latest book.'

'I didn't know she was a friend of yours.' Maddy sounded wary.

'Well, I wouldn't . . .' I paused, suddenly awake to the implications. 'Oh yes, I've known Gilly for years.' I waited to see if I'd got it right.

'Darling!' Maddy managed, then quickly, 'Of course you know I'd never make trouble for anyone but she told *lies* about me, Micky, in her book. Jessica told me. Lies about Angela and me.'

'How did she come to do that?' I wondered how Maddy's powers of imagination were functioning at the moment. They were pretty good, as it happened.

'Well, the silliest mistake, really. Angela met that—Miss Fry—at a party and told her a really sad story about a friend of hers. That—Miss Fry—used the story in her book but thought Angela had been talking about *herself!*' She

laughed again, amused, charming. 'How could she have
thought such a thing! Well, I told her, naturally I couldn't
allow her to print it. I have to protect my little girl. She's
such an innocent. It could damage Angela's reputation, you
know.'

'Gillian said you hit Angela,' I said bluntly.

'Oh no, how could she?'

'Tony Ridgeway told me the same thing this morning.
Said you had a row with Angela last night and hit her.'

'Micky! It was an *accident*, really! I was feeling awfully ill
and had such a terrible headache and Angela said something that upset me very much. I only slapped her. I'm her
mother and I do believe in discipline. Angela's still a child.
You don't realize what it's like these days, all the tempta-
tions girls face. Angel's too young to decide things for herself.' She waited a moment, then went on quickly, 'I
promised Morgan I'd bring her up with every advantage
and look after her just as well as he would himself.'

'Perhaps she's wiser than you give her credit for,' I countered. 'You could try listening to her, Maddy.'

'You really must accept that I know my Angel better
than you do. She's my child, after all. She may seem quite
mature but in some ways she's still just my baby. Now,
Micky,' her voice was soft, caressing, 'don't let's argue
about it. You'll see I'm right in the end.'

I knew better than to try. Even Morgan couldn't change
Maddy. He'd learned to compromise and live with it. But
I knew he would have drawn the line at Maddy physically
hurting Angela and he'd have been on hand to stop her. I
was angry that I'd never noticed it going on, if Maddy was
making a habit of it—and I was the one who prided myself
on keeping a fatherly eye on the girl! A little stab of worry
went through me. I wondered if just by mentioning Gillian
I could be causing Angela trouble. I tried again, feeling as
if I was walking on eggshells.

'What about Gillian? I've suggested she alter the central

character in the book. Would you take the heat off her if she agrees?'

She sounded honestly regretful. 'You see how it is. She really is determined to damage us and I could never trust her not to tell lies in another book. Anyway, have you *read* her books? They're quite awful. Depressing and ugly and immoral. They shouldn't be allowed. Young people are so impressionable. She's got them all believing she's wonderful and lapping up her disgusting trash. I can't see why she's so popular. You'd think children would prefer something happy and wholesome.'

Like *Kids' World*, I thought, and realized with a shock that Maddy was jealous of Gillian's success. Apparently anyone with a youthful following was a dangerous rival to be stopped at all costs. I felt sick and out of my depth. Some Galahad! I had no idea how to slay this particular dragon. I tried another tack.

'What does Gwen think about it?' Gwen was Maddy's agent.

'Oh, Gwen,' she said impatiently, 'she's as bad as the rest. Actually, I'm dropping her. She's been giving Angel all sorts of unsuitable ideas behind my back—filling her head with a lot of rubbish about taking a part in *Kids' World*. Angela's totally unsuited to the world of television. She's just not up to the work and the politicking that goes on behind the scenes. She's too fragile and immature. Now Gwen is encouraging her to write! She's hopeless, and the pity of it is that she believes she's quite good because Gwen told her. Angela always wants to copy me, do what I do, and she just doesn't have the talent, poor child. I've told Gwen that I'm terminating our contract. I've a dozen agents wanting to represent me. I don't need Gwen Bright!'

I'd already failed in my attempts to help first Gillian and then Angela. I felt defending Gwen would make it three in a row. I decided to shut up and managed to excuse myself from joining Maddy for dinner any night in the near future.

CHAPTER 7

I was fully occupied for most of the following week with publicity for *Winifred Joins the Chorus*. Alan's publicity department had done its usual efficient job and I buzzed around the city from one interview to another. On Monday a box of extremely expensive handmade chocolates arrived from Chocs, with a gilt-edged card signed by Maddy being true to form. She was on deck at the studio again and I was booked to be interviewed by her on Wednesday for *Kids' World*. I fronted up to the channel, conscious of the receptionist's scrutiny, was collected speedily from the waiting area and ushered up the stairs to the first floor into make-up, where an attractive girl whose name tag proclaimed her as Lenore made my face acceptable to the camera.

There was a heated conversation beyond a connecting door marked 'Ironing Room'. A vaguely familiar woman's voice was going on about something and was answered from time to time by soothing murmurs, accompanied by the hiss of a steam iron and the hot scent of just-ironed clothes.

'So you write children's books?' Lenore said brightly. 'That must be interesting.'

I caught the words, 'She's used me, just used me. Ever since I can remember.'

'Where do you get your ideas from?' Lenore patted at the crease between my brows.

'Oh, here and there,' I said absently.

'Well, I think you writers are so clever, always coming up with something new.'

'. . . to just dump me like that after all these years. Who

got her all her chances? She'd never have met Morgan Grey
if I hadn't fought for her . . .'

'Have you done a TV interview before?'

'A few.' I knew who it was now and my stomach cringed.
Not more drama, I pleaded silently. I might have known
the god of trouble would be lurking around the studio.

'Well, you'll be fine, then. It's a good programme today.'

The outer door opened and a tall man with dark hair,
flecked with silver, entered and smiled at Lenore. 'Room
for one more?' He nodded at me and took the second chair.

'Oh, Frank, Gracie's been waiting for you.' She gave a
call towards the ironing room, the voices cut off abruptly
and a pretty, willowy blonde girl appeared in the doorway.

'Frank. You're taping the *Earth Report* at three, is that
right?'

'Well, one day someone's going to give that bitch exactly
what she deserves and I hope I'm there to see it!'

The blonde looked startled and quickly pulled the door
shut. Her eyes met Lenore's and they exchanged a knowing
grin.

'Don't tell me you girls are gossiping in there again.' The
dark-haired man smiled at me in the long mirror over the
make-up table as Gracie tucked a paper towel into his col-
lar. Then his smile deepened.

'Hello! Don't I know you?'

'Micky Douglas,' I supplied. 'We met a couple of months
ago at a party at Maddy Grey's.'

'Of course, you're the writer.' He held out his hand and
gripped mine. 'I suppose you're doing an interview with
her.'

Frank Young read the evening news and was something
of a heart throb among the ladies of Brisbane. Monica told
me once it was because he had 'a gorgeous voice, and eyes
like a sad puppy'. I glanced surreptitiously at his face
receiving its coating of artificial tan, although it hardly
needed it, but his eyes were closed.

'There you go, Mr Douglas. Do you know the way to the studio? Just along the corridor and you can go right in and wait in there.'

Frank Young opened his eyes. They were large, brown and certainly spaniel-like.

'I'll see you, Frank.'

'Later, Micky.'

He'd been at the party alone and had been quickly surrounded by women. I'd noticed Maddy covertly watching him, occasionally teasing him and flirting, and wondered why his wife hadn't come, if only to keep an eye on him. Maddy had laughed at the suggestion.

'Poor little Jasmine? She's just a mouse. Never goes out to parties. I can't think why Frank ever married her, she's hardly a companion for him. She'll be sitting at home watching some boring romance on TV and waiting up for Frank. What a life! She'll be lucky if someone doesn't walk off with that lovely hunk right under her dowdy little nose.'

They'd tried, but Frank had gone home to his wife promptly at midnight, in spite of Maddy calling him 'Cinderella'.

Maddy was at her charming best and the studio audience was enthusiastic. I was kept signing autographs for a time afterwards while they changed the set. There was no sign of Angela, although Bobby West was in the studio looking subdued, only bouncing to life when he was before the cameras, caught in the glare of the lights. Wes Martin looked harassed as usual, although Maddy was behaving beautifully with professional ease.

I had no time for a private conversation with her except to thank her for the chocolates, although I'd been tempted to chuck them out of the window.

'I felt I had to do something to make up for last Saturday. And I'm going to launch your book, of course. I'm looking forward to it. It's Monday night, isn't it? Perhaps you'll let me make another announcement, too, that Winifred Wombat is about to become a TV star.'

Thankfully, I wasn't given the chance to reply. Wes called for quiet and Maddy's smile glinted into the camera as the auto cue began to roll through my introduction. I escaped without further incident and visited the make-up room on the way out to wash my face.

By Friday the hoop-la was all but over and I was able to relax. I called Gillian and explained it was 'no dice' with Maddy.

'She can't do it. She can't hound me and make my life a misery.' Gillian sounded desperate. 'Someone should stop her. She's loathsome.' I couldn't think of anything comforting to say and hoped she wouldn't decide to confront Maddy on Monday night. I thought optimistically: She's got three days to calm down; surely she'll be OK. She must see she'll have to change the bloody book! Then Maddy won't have a leg to stand on.

On Saturday morning I took the Capri up the road to Paddo's 7-2-7 and restocked the food cupboard, then settled down to some much needed housework. No. 18 was unusually quiet. Malcolm Pryce, basement flat, was on tour with his ballet company somewhere up north, Deirdre Carstairs, Flat 1, was in Sydney at a computer conference, and Peta Ryde, Flat 4, was on holiday in the Kakadu National Park. There was no sign of Monica, either. She visited her mother on Saturdays and often stayed the night. From my kitchen window I could see Al Wang from Flat 3 talking to Carnie in the back garden. The sun was shining, the jacaranda trees in the park across the road were stunning the senses with their shock of mauve blossoms, my duty to the publicity machine was done and all was well in my peaceful world. Until the phone rang.

I told my caller he was welcome to come around; no, I

wasn't particularly busy, yes, half an hour would be fine, no, I didn't mind.

With a sinking feeling in my heart I put a pot of coffee on to brew.

CHAPTER 8

Bobby West sipped his coffee and sorted out his thoughts. I waited. My sense of foreboding had increased at the sight of his troubled face.

'Angela talks about you a lot,' he said and smiled apologetically. 'It's about her, you probably guessed.'

'I probably did,' I said evenly.

'She says you've been a real friend to her, ever since her father died. I never knew Morgan Grey but he sounds like a good man. I can't understand why he married Maddy,' he added, half to himself.

I grinned. 'You're not alone there, but in spite of what you might hear, Morgan loved Maddy very much and understood her better than anyone. But you didn't come to talk about Maddy.'

He looked at me, his pleasant face clouded. 'I'm fond of Angela,' he told me bluntly.

'I know it.'

'Don't get the wrong idea. There's nothing between us except friendship. She's only fourteen. But—but—I'm pretty much in love with her, if you want the truth.'

'You haven't told her?'

'What do you take me for? I reckon she knows it, though.'

'I think you're right. What are you going to do about it?'

'Nothing. What can I do? I'm ten years older than she is, you know. But I'm fully prepared to wait until she's old enough to speak to and then, well, we'll see how she feels.'

I suddenly felt like an ageing cupid, helpless in the face

of such confident young love. He seemed to have it all
worked out, anyway.

'She's very mature for her age. Well, I mean, being
Maddy's daughter, what can you expect?'

'Bobby, forgive me for sounding like an elderly cynic but
you're a young, successful, good-looking bloke and don't
tell me you don't have the girls after you. What makes you
think you'll feel the same way in two or three years?'

'Point taken,' he said frankly, 'but that's been the case
for a long time now and I've never fallen for any of them.
I've had chicks, sure, but I've never been in love.'

'You were pretty keen on Maddy four years ago,' I said
drily.

He flushed. 'Yes, I was totalled by her. She was so beautiful and sophisticated and like a—a grieving Madonna after
Morgan died—and she paid me a lot of attention. Well, I
was only twenty—didn't have a clue! I was infatuated by
her for months and flattered and thought I was really something to have won on to Maddy Grey! Then I began to see
what she was like and I was sick. My God!' He groaned
and shook his head in disbelief. 'She used me pretty well
how she liked and I was too stupid to suss her out. When
I did, I couldn't get away. I was contracted to *Kids' World*,
seeing her every day. She's like a spider.' In spite of the
heat of the day he shivered slightly. 'She spins a web around
you and coats it with honey and you get so stuck you can't
get out. The worst thing is, she can treat you like dirt, make
a fool out of you, behave like the world's prize bitch and
then make you feel it's all your fault. I used to come back
apologizing to her and telling her how sorry I was when all
the time it was down to her . . . ! God, I was a crass berk!
I tried to leave her. It was like, a—a sort of insanity. She's
very addictive—but then, you'd know that.'

I shook my head and poured him another cuppa. 'She's
not my type. I never understood how she gets away with it
or how she suckers so many blokes. She's always been very

careful around me for that reason, I think. She could never do to me whatever it is she does do.'

'You're lucky.' He shuddered again. 'If she hadn't met some other bloke I don't know what I'd have done. She threw me over and it hurt like hell. I was a mess. It was as if I'd been, I don't know, dazzled by the sun, I suppose, and then plunged into the dark. Dazzled? Blinded, more like. But then, after a time, I could see again and Angela was there. I think she liked me and we always got on really well. She was sorry for me. She knew what was going on—you can't fool her where her mother's concerned. And I just—fell in love with her. She's sweet and gentle and generous. Then I knew I'd never been in love with Maddy at all. Just—just bowled over by her. There was nothing left in my feelings for her. Angela's the best and I reckon she's worth waiting for.'

I looked him over in silence. He certainly had all the symptoms. His eyes were shining, his voice softened when he mentioned Angela, his face had a glowing look. I sighed. I could only see major trouble ahead for them both.

'Bobby, why are you telling me all this?' I asked. I knew I wouldn't like the answer. I was right.

'It's Maddy,' he confided, a worried frown settling on his forehead. 'I think she's guessed. She had some Channel 6 people over for dinner last night. Angela's got exams soon and she was having problems with maths. I've always been pretty good, although it's a while since I did any, and I offered to help out. We went off to her study. We were sitting together on the lounge—not doing anything, just talking. She told me about the row with Gillian Fry and she was crying. I put my arm around her, just for comfort, I wasn't about to take advantage, and, well, you can guess, Maddy chose that of all moments to come in.'

'Hell!' I could picture the scene. 'How did she react?'

Bobby looked puzzled. 'Surprisingly calmly,' he said slowly. 'She said she'd just popped in to see if we needed anything and she told me to go back to the others and she'd

look after Angela. I wasn't about to leave them alone but
Angela signalled me to go. Maddy was chattering on and
soothing her but her face looked—frozen. Like she'd had a
shock. She came back to the party about ten minutes later
and said Angela had gone to bed. She was really sweet to
me. She told me not to take Angela's stories too seriously.
She didn't fly into a temper or anything.'

Now it was my turn to look worried. I'd seen Maddy go
through almost every sort of tantrum in the book. Self-
control was not her style. I wondered what she was up to.

'Are you sure she suspected how you felt about Angela?'

'She couldn't have missed it,' Bobby said simply. 'We
were sort of—looking at each other. We couldn't look away.
I think Angela had just realized how I felt about her and
she . . . Micky—' his eyes were bright—'she feels the same
way. I'm sure of it!'

'Yes,' I said, and I couldn't match his enthusiasm. 'I
know she does. No, she didn't tell me. It's fairly obvious,
I'm afraid.'

He was silent, presumably thinking about the moment when
love had stirred between them. My stomach twisted. I wasn't
optimistic that love would conquer all. I could see Angela being
sent away, Bobby being sacked from the show . . .

'I rang her this morning.' He'd come back to earth. 'She
said Maddy was very quiet, had been on the phone all
morning and working with her secretary. She thought something was up but didn't know why Maddy hadn't taken it
out on her, thank goodness.'

Give her time, I thought.

'So I wanted to talk to you. Angela says you sort of look
out for her and I thought you'd spot it right away if Maddy
was hurting her. You seem to be able to deal with her better
than anyone—well, according to Angela.'

How did I get this reputation for being able to handle
Spider Woman, I thought irritably. Anyway, I didn't even
realize Maddy was hurting her at all. I'm worse than

useless. I heard myself reassuring Bobby, promising to do whatever I could if Maddy turned nasty, wondering if there really was a lump of cold steel in my gut.

He left, looking much more cheerful. 'Angela needs all the friends she can get right now. Thanks, Micky. I'm sure it will all work out.'

'Cockeyed—bloody—optimist!' I told the door as it closed behind him. 'What the hell's going on?' There was an impatient scratching on the other side and I opened it again. 'Sorry, Carnie, didn't see you there, love. So, what do you think's happening, Princess?'

She gave a wide yawn, said, 'Frankly, Micky, I couldn't care less,' ran gracefully up the short flight of stairs to the open mezzanine floor which I use as a bedroom and appropriated my bed for a late morning nap.

The rest of the weekend was uneventful. On Monday morning I phoned Riley's to check all was going smoothly for that night. 'Maddy seems to be OK,' I told John. 'She sounded pretty happy about the launch on Wednesday.'

'I wish we'd never asked her.' John's voice sounded tight, over-tense.

'Don't worry, John. She'll do a good job. She wants Winifred rather badly.'

'It's not that.' He hesitated, then said, 'What the hell, it'll be all over town by tonight anyway. She's dumped us, Micky. The bloody woman's dropped us right in it!'

'What's happened?' I thought: Bloody hell, here it comes. I was right again.

'She rang me first thing this morning. I'd barely got the shop open. She's withdrawing the franchise for *Kids' World* next month.'

'Eh? She can't!'

'Oh yes she can, mate. We were to renew the agreement by the end of this month. Now it seems she's done a deal with Gaby Mentos. She's signed a contract to take *Kids' World* to Channel 8. They have their own market outlets, the

Super 8 shops, and they want the *Kids' World* merchandise. We're right out of it, Micky.'

I was stunned, although something inside had warned me it was coming. John's voice was bitter.

'I don't know what we're going to do now. I'd like to strangle her!'

It seemed to be universal. Hell! I thought wearily. It's going to be a merry bloody book launch. I felt like doing the world a favour and murdering Maddy myself.

CHAPTER 9

It was clear that no act of God or anyone else was about to stop the book launch going ahead, although I might have welcomed some divine intervention. A few clouds hanging about on Monday morning had pushed off by midday, leaving the sky uniformly blue from horizon to horizon. Even if it had rained buckets John would have simply moved the whole affair inside the shop. It had happened before.

The launch was five-thirty for six, early enough for children to stay up for. I was due at five to sign books and socialize with the invited guests as they arrived. I drove up to Riley's ten minutes before the hour, just in time to grab a park directly outside the front door.

Tonight Riley's belonged to me. On the pavement by the entrance, a notice board carried a large poster advertising the launch and a full-size photograph of my face smiled out at the street. A table just inside was covered with my books, pride of place given to *Winifred Joins the Chorus*, the volumes cleverly stacked into a pyramid by Fiona, who was behind the counter serving some late customers.

'Micky.' She gave me a kiss under the interested gaze of a couple of males waiting to make their purchases. Fiona's a pretty girl. 'Dad's downstairs. You heard the news?'

'Yes, John told me earlier.'

'He's fairly shattered,' she said in my ear. 'I've never seen him so—crushed. I wish I could do something to change that awful woman's mind.' She darted back to the counter. 'Go on down,' she told me, 'everything's set up. Yes, sir, can I help you?'

I gave her a wave and made my way down to the office. John was on the phone, as usual, and nodded a welcome, pointing me out on to the verandah where Barbara was sitting at a table piled high with Winifred's latest adventure. She was gazing unseeingly out across the garden, her face sombre. I bent over and kissed her cheek and she jumped and turned to me. Her eyes were moist.

'He tries so hard,' she said in a low voice. 'Oh, we all do our bit, but John, he *is* Riley's, heart and soul. He's built it up over the years, made it a success, given all the family a place. He's hung on, in spite of this damned recession, he's worked and slaved every day of the week to hold it all together. And now this!' She dashed an impatient hand across her eyes. 'It isn't fair, Micky.'

'Surely there're sales enough to put the *Kids' World* merchandise into the Super 8 shops as well as Riley's,' I wondered aloud. 'Maddy wouldn't miss the chance to double her money. Does she have an exclusive contract with 8? It doesn't sound like her.'

'She's doing it for pure spite,' Barbara said indignantly. 'She's annoyed because we had Gillian Fry here for an evening. She said she didn't approve of the sort of people we supported. Practically accused us of corrupting the minds of young people by having Gilly's books in the shop.'

'Ah!' That did sound like Maddy. 'But she's launching Winifred here.'

'Oh, she'd do anything for you,' Barbara snapped. 'Until she gets Winifred for *Kids' World* you can't do a thing wrong.'

I grinned at her sympathetically and she looked contrite.

'I'm sorry. What an awful thing to say. Don't worry about us, Micky, we'll come about. We're not as badly off as some. The people next door are moving out next month when their lease is up. Antiques just aren't making enough to pay the rent.'

I was sorry. I liked the little antique shop which was separated from Riley's by a narrow strip of ground, mostly taken up by an old wooden paling fence. Both shops were owned by the same man and the antique shop had also been restored to Original Pioneer. They made a nice matched set.

Barbara got me to work signing books. People began to drift down the stairs and, after a brief chat and introduction, were passed on down the next flight to the garden below where Don waited with drinks and nibbles. It was another few weeks to daylight saving so the light had begun to fade. Barbara left me to handle the people and went into the office to switch on the terrace lights which were set in short posts along the winding path leading to the white latticed gazebo at the bottom of the garden.

A couple of youngsters claimed my attention and had brought their favourite and much read Winifred books for me to sign. I assured their mother I didn't mind in the least and was listening to the story of a wombat they'd seen at a wildlife sanctuary when Tony Ridgeway appeared on the verandah with Bobby West and Angela. All three looked slightly dazed and Tony gave me a frantic signal. I excused myself and went over to them, fearing the worst. The worst came.

'It's Maddy,' Tony hissed. 'She's drunk again.'

I shot a quick look at Bobby. He was holding Angela's hand protectively. She looked as if she'd been crying.

'Bobby, take Angela down and get yourselves a drink. Don does a fruit punch second to none.'

Bobby threw me a grateful look and ushered Angela away.

'What the hell!' I began softly.

'Don't ask me,' Tony said in a furious undertone. 'Have you heard what's been going on? God knows why! She was right as rain all week, then today she went off the rails completely. She's taken out a lawsuit against Jessica Savage for libel, walked out on Channel 6, signed with Gaby Mentos for *Kids' World*, sacked Bobby from the show and apparently pulled the *Kids' World* franchise out from under Riley's feet. Not bad for one day's work!'

'You said she couldn't take the show,' I hissed, smiling and waving at some people who were trying to catch my eye.

'She can't. I'm damned sure of it. Her solicitor is going mad trying to calm her down.'

'We can't talk here.' I was seething. 'Bloody hell, Tony, who's supposed to do the launch now?'

'She says she can do it.' He shrugged. 'She's out in the car with Gwen. She's still upright and fairly lucid although she's been hitting the bottle all afternoon.'

'What do you reckon?'

'I just don't know. Christ! What a bloody mess. She's been advertised and a lot of people will be coming just to see her.'

I let that go by. It was probably true. I looked at my watch.

'It's half an hour to the launch. Can you get her in? Sober her up?'

Barbara appeared and cast a startled glance at the people waiting for their books to be signed. 'What's wrong, Micky?'

'One guess, Babs,' I groaned. 'Maddy's on another binge. Can we slip her into the office and try to sober her up before the launch?'

She compressed her lips angrily. For her it was the last straw. That went for me, too.

'All right, Tony, go inside and get John to give you a

hand in with her. Micky, you'd better get back to the people
and let us handle this. This is supposed to be a celebration
of your book,' she wailed softly. 'I'll make some extra black
coffee and I hope it chokes her!'

I held the fort, chatting with Winifred's fans and signing
their books. Fiona appeared magically to handle the money.

'Mum sent me down,' she whispered. 'That bloody cow
Maddy! How dare she do this to you!'

'Tony reckons she's capable of making a speech. Your
mum's trying to sober her up with coffee. We'll just have
to cross our fingers.'

Rebecca Roland made a glamorous entrance and drew
'oohs' from the growing crowd. She gave me a surreptitious
'thumbs up' sign as she passed and I saw her go down to
Angela and put an arm around her. Gillian Fry came down
from the shop and bought a book.

'Write something special in it,' she giggled. I resisted the
impulse to write 'something special' and managed a suit-
able little tribute. 'Is it true?' she whispered, leaning over
me. 'I saw Maddy Grey come in. She's supposed to be blind
drunk in the office.'

'I think she's OK now,' I told her. 'Barbara's feeding her
coffee.'

'They should let her fall on her face,' Gillian said vindic-
tively, 'except that it would hurt you. One day there won't
be anyone there to pick her up. Then . . . Oh gosh! There's
Jessica Savage.' She gave a startled gasp and fled down the
stairs into the garden.

Jessica, slim and elegant in a black suit which set off her
copper hair, her shapely legs stunningly displayed in black
stockings, gave me a knowing wink but all she said was,
'Congrats again, Michael. I must say you're an inspiration
to us all,' and followed the drift to the garden.

A small group came out on to the verandah and I recognized Karen Blair among them and one of the barrel girls.
This must be the promised offering from Channel 6. I

noticed with surprise the tall, handsome figure of Frank Young and he joined me, smiling charmingly at Fiona as he paid out for the book.

'Mine are a little too young to bring along,' he told me, 'but I'm under orders from Jasmine to say they love your books, Micky. Will you sign this to Jason and Megan?' He dropped his voice. 'Is Maddy all right?'

'Does everybody know what's going on?' I asked crossly.

'Only the people from the channel.' He shrugged. 'After what she's been up to today they could hardly not. We've got wall to wall legal people up at the studios, Tracey Whitehead's run off her feet and looking distinctly harassed, and Gwenny Bright's going demented. Poor Maddy.'

'Poor *Maddy?*' I echoed.

'Don't you think she's rather more to be pitied than despised? No? She can't cope, you know. The pressure of being Number One is always destructive, doubly so to her. She's like a little girl, wanting everyone to like her and be pleased with her. I'd call that a pretty sad situation. She's her own worst enemy.' He gave another slight shrug and turned away.

'Well, that's another way of looking at it,' Fiona said tartly.

I checked my watch again. Ten to six. Fiona patted my hand.

'Give them time. They'll be watching the clock in there. Dad'll be out to give us a report soon.'

I smiled feebly at her. I was not a happy person. However, a minute later, John and Barbara hurried out of the office looking decidedly more relaxed.

'She'll do,' Barbara said with relief. 'She's very apologetic and she's just touching up her face. She's all nerves but Tony says it's normal for her before she speaks in public.'

Gwen Bright's short, plump figure hovered for a moment in the office doorway, then she too came across the

verandah, peering at us short-sightedly through her thick
glasses.

'Tony's waiting with her and he'll bring her down. I'm
so sorry, Micky. She's been like a mad thing all day but
she seems quite calm now.'

'We'd better go down.' John touched my arm and we
descended the stairs into the garden, making our way
around the groups of people who chattered and ate and
drank and called out to late arriving friends. As we moved
down to the gazebo, pausing briefly to talk with this one
and that, the crowd gathered closer, finding places to sit on
the benches or the sets of brick steps linking the terraces or
standing in a knot at the back. I saw Angela, Bobby and
Rebecca leave an admiring group and move to a bench half
way down the garden, their faces indistinct in the deepening
shadows. Dusk was settling all around us and the cicadas
were striking up their evening chorus, a high-pitched buzz
which would go on for hours. The air was perfumed with
the scent of honeysuckle from a vine along the back fence
and a couple of extra large spiders hung low in a tall euca-
lypt, taking advantage of the lights which would lure many
unwary moths.

John and I reached the gazebo where John had set up
chairs and a table with a copy of my book, a jug of iced
water and a microphone. We both cast an anxious look
towards the shop to see Tony hurrying down the stairs. As
he came closer we could see the black look on his face. We
both tensed as he reached us.

'She's welched!' he said in a savage whisper. 'Says she
won't do it. I've tried to reason with her but it's hopeless.
You'll have to manage without her!'

CHAPTER 10

John Riley has organized more book launches than he can count and is used to handling last-minute emergencies. In fact, he'll keep you entertained for hours with disaster stories although at the time they weren't so amusing. Now he turned quickly to Tony.

'Can you do the launch?'

'I'm not in the public eye. What about Becky?'

'Go and ask her, will you? I'll start things moving.'

Tony nodded and picked his way around the waiting people. I sat down weakly while John took up the microphone and began a short speech of welcome. I saw Tony reach the others and begin a hurried conversation. Angela jumped up and looked back to the shop as if about to run to her mother but Bobby pulled her down beside him. Becky got to her feet and followed her husband through the crowd, smiling and apologizing. There was a note of relief in John's voice as he saw her and wound up his speech, calling upon the audience to welcome Rebecca Rowland, popular star of *Summer Days*, and she moved into the light and took the microphone with practised aplomb. John joined me at the back of the gazebo and we both crossed our fingers. It was unnecessary. Becky launched into her impromptu introduction sounding as if she'd prepared it weeks ago. It seemed she'd worked in another TV drama which had a wombat as a central character and whether her stories were fact or created on the spot, she certainly had her audience in stitches, proving what I'd always known—that behind her empty-headed sex symbol character, Amanda Drake, was a cool intelligent and highly efficient woman, Rebecca Ridgeway.

While Becky delighted her audience my attention kept

straying to the back of the garden. Tony had retreated to the rear of the crowd, his fair head visible above the rest. Jessica Savage remained half way down the stairs and I could pick her out clearly, her copper hair glinting in the bright lamp that spotlighted the area. I forced myself to look at Becky and concentrate on what she was saying. When I glanced back, Jessica had disappeared.

Becky wound up and handed me the microphone, joining John at the back of the gazebo. I waited for the applause to die down. Gillian Fry's tall figure was now illuminated on the back stairs, coming down to the garden where there was a movement of people towards the refreshment table, taking advantage of the pause. I took a deep breath and began to talk about Winifred. I was just getting into my stride when I heard a door slam and looked up again involuntarily, nerves on the twitch. Fiona had come out of the office and in the verandah light I could see her wiping her eyes with a handkerchief. Jessica, now back on the verandah, watched as Fiona stumbled to the second flight of steps and ran up them to the shop. I caught the thread of what I'd been saying and ploughed on. If I could last the distance without losing my sanity I figured I'd be doing well. The audience laughed responsively as I attempted a joke.

A minute later my worst fears were realized. Out of the corner of my eye I spotted movement on the verandah and Maddy appeared, clutching at the doorway. My heart sank as I watched the unsteady figure making her way down the stairs, hand over hand on the rails, bumping into Jessica who moved disdainfully aside. I forced myself to keep lightly chatting and nearly gave a sigh of relief as Maddy stumbled against Tony, who grabbed her and began to lead her to some chairs at the very back of the garden under a stand of tall tree ferns, away from the crowd which had pressed forward again when I'd begun to talk. They seemed to be having an altercation but, thankfully, another burst of laughter masked any other sound as I stuck doggedly to my task. Tony's blond head appeared by the drinks table and then moved back to the deep shadows where he'd left Maddy.

I glanced at my watch. Too soon to stop. I felt trapped in the sticky threads of a nightmare and was thankful when Tony became visible again and signalled an 'all clear'. Reassured, I battled brightly on, quite in the Winifred tradition, determined to do my bit to make the evening a success.

I noticed Jessica had moved back down the stairs and was just above Frank Young and Gillian Fry who were standing together. Fiona came down from the shop to help serve the guests who'd stay on after the official business of the launch to rub shoulders with the celebrities and socialize some more. There was no sign of Maddy, thank God, and at last the slow hands of my watch were telling me I'd done my duty and could hand back to John.

'And so, Winifred Wombat joined the chorus,' I told the listening crowd, 'but that was just the start of her adventures. To find out what happens . . .' I held up the book suggestively and got another laugh.

John got to his feet and took the mike. I whispered, 'Maddy's on the loose but I think it's OK. Tony seems to have managed her.'

'Damn!' John hissed back. 'He'd better have!' And began his final comments, calling once more for a round of applause. It came willingly and a man half way down the garden raised his hand.

'Will Winifred ever get out of the chorus and be a star?' he asked. Everybody laughed. More questions followed. A small child came confidently down to the front.

'Is Winifred really real?' he asked in a clear voice.

'What do you think?' I countered.

He ran back shouting, 'Mum, Winifred *is* real!' and the laughter broke out again.

John ended the question session to a final burst of

applause, then I was settled at the table in the gazebo for
more signing and private questions from Winifred's fans.
The groups began to break up, people mingled, parents left
with tired children. Angela ran up the stairs to the office. I
assumed she hadn't realized Maddy had come down and
was probably out to it again. I couldn't see what was happening in the dark back corner. A few minutes later Bobby
West made his way over to Maddy. Tony was now with
Rebecca, chatting to a group gathered around his lovely
wife. Maddy must be out like a light. I had a line-up of
people at the table and prayed she'd stay that way until the
guests had all left. Then we could bring her around and get
her home. Bobby came back into the light and moved
quickly down the garden. In the back of my mind was the
ever present fear that Maddy's latest binge had been
brought on by finding him and Angela together.

When I had time to look up again, the crowd had thinned
considerably and I was free to move into the garden, get
myself an urgently needed drink and mingle. Bobby was
now signing autographs, surrounded by young fans. Angela
watched him from the shadows, a troubled look on her face.
Frank Young was charming a group of women and even
Gillian Fry was signing a copy of one of her books. I
breathed easier. Fiona saw me on the move and brought
me a glass of wine and a tray of nibbles. I helped myself
thankfully. She was pale and her smile obviously cost her
an effort.

'Perk up, Sunshine,' I told her. 'Nearly over now. I
gather Maddy's still under control?'

Fiona pulled a face. 'She's unconscious in a corner, thank
goodness. Did you see?'

'"Most everything,"' I said, using one of Winifred's
favourite expressions. 'Maybe a poisonous spider will get
her.'

'In our garden? I hope not! No one would ever come to
a book launch again. Anyway, we don't get red-backs or

funnelwebs, I'm glad to say, and she'd probably survive anything else—or poison them!'

She seemed a little restored and I joined Gwen Bright who waved at me. Don Riley was now working around the garden, gathering discarded cups. John was in the gazebo winding up the microphone cord. I noticed Gillian still talking earnestly with some teenagers.

Gwen and I joined the slow movement up to the back of the garden. People drank a last wine, called good night. We joined Frank Young and the Ridgeways and I put my arm around Becky and hugged her.

'You wonderful thing, you.'

She laughed. 'Was I OK?'

'You were superb!'

'You were pretty good yourself.'

Tony grinned, his relief in victory snatched from the jaws of disaster tangible. 'Is this a mutual admiration society or can anyone join in?'

'Thanks, Tony!' I smiled back at him. 'You saved the day pretty well yourself.'

'Lucky I was there. I gather you saw La Grey come staggering down the stairs. She wanted to go down and join in the launch. I'm sorry to say I had to give her a glass of wine to shut her up and she passed out again. I couldn't think of anything else to do. She was quite violent and abusive.' Although he'd begun to relax, his face was still showing the strain of the evening's events.

'She brings it on herself,' Becky said shortly. 'I hear she's walked out on you, Gwenny.'

'Oh—' Gwen's eyes were large behind her thick lenses —'she doesn't mean it. You'll see, she'll ask me back. Poor Maddy, she'll be so sorry later. It was my fault, really.'

Becky cast up her eyes at me.

Gillian was hovering in the background. She looked tired and rather wilted.

'I just wanted to say goodbye, Micky, and I'm so pleased for you.'

'Thanks, Gilly.'

Bobby and Angela came up. 'Is Mum all right?' Angela asked. Her voice was weary and shook slightly. Gillian moved towards her in an uncertain way and Tony put an arm around the girl.

'She's asleep, Angie. She'll be OK.'

Angela gave him a quick, nervous look. 'Thanks, Tony. We'd better get her home.'

'I'll go and wake her up,' Frank said abruptly and walked across the paving to the back corner of the shrubbery where Maddy could just be seen slumped in a chair.

Tony released Angela. 'I'll give him a hand.' Frank was bending over Maddy and shaking her gently. 'Why don't you take Angie home, Bobby? Gwen and Becky and I will look after Maddy.'

'I'll wait.' Angela was watching Frank as he came back into the light. His face was white and he swallowed several times.

'I—I can't wake her,' he said in a shocked voice. 'Sh—she's—dead!'

There was a stunned silence. 'She can't be,' Bobby said reasonably. Gwen gave a little cry and went towards Maddy but Frank held her back.

'I'm sorry. She is dead.'

Gillian suddenly screamed. We all jumped and she covered her mouth with her hand. I looked at Angela. She was motionless, her face taut. She glanced towards Bobby and he reached out a hand. She gripped it tightly.

'Oh Christ!' Tony was staring at Frank. Then suddenly he was galvanized into action. He tried to push past Frank who said simply, 'No, Tony, don't. She shouldn't be touched.'

'You don't understand!' he said frantically. 'If she's dead, I killed her!'

CHAPTER 11

We sat crowded together in the office. I looked around at the faces which were registering a confused range of emotions. Tony was slumped in a chair, his hands over his eyes. He hadn't spoken since his dramatic outburst. Beside him, Becky, looking bewildered, kept a comforting hand on his arm. Angela and Bobby were perched on a table, her face hidden in his shoulder, his arm around her, his expression fiercely protective. Gillian Fry, looking frightened, sat in a corner. Don Riley moved quietly in the kitchen next door, washing plates and putting food away. Fiona, shocked and confused, sat at her desk, Frank Young stood leaning against the wall. He looked ill and I wondered if he was going to throw up. Every now and then he gave an involuntary shudder. His face was still as white as a sheet. Gwen Bright sobbed uncontrollably and Barbara Riley handed her tissues in a helpless way and made soothing noises.

John Riley had stepped forward as Tony made his shocking statement and had taken control. He'd moved a protesting Frank aside and had bent over Maddy, feeling for her pulse. He'd returned looking grave and told us there was nothing we could do. Maddy was beyond help.

'There's a surgery just down the road. They'll still be open. Don, go and get a doctor. The rest of us had better move inside. Come on, it won't help standing around here.'

We followed him like zombies, dazed at the turn of events. Within minutes the doctor had arrived and John had taken him into the garden, leaving us to wait, too obviously avoiding one another's eyes for what seemed an age while Gwen's lamentations went on.

Footsteps sounded on the verandah and John entered the office. His face had lost its stoic calm and wore an expression of disbelief. He was followed by the white clad doctor who put down his bag and looked sternly around the room.

'This is Dr Edgely,' John said quietly. 'Doctor, that's Tony Ridgeway.'

Tony lifted his face and met Edgely's gaze. The doctor spoke sharply.

'Mr Riley tells me you claimed to have killed Mrs Grey.'

'It must have been me.' He spoke jerkily as if the words were forced out of him. 'I didn't tell you everything before.' He looked frantically around at the faces watching him. 'I didn't just give Maddy a glass of wine. I had some sleeping tablets with me. I always keep them for emergencies like— like tonight. When I could see she was working herself up to a fury I slipped a couple into her wine and they worked almost instantly. She—she just collapsed. I thought she was asleep. It must have been too much on top of all the alcohol she'd had. It must have killed her. I never meant to.' His eyes were fixed on the doctor, his voice pleading.

Dr Edgely raised his eyebrows and said briskly, 'Good God, man, she didn't die from sleeping tablets. Who found the body?'

Frank lurched forward slightly. 'I did.'

'Well, didn't you notice anything out of order?'

Frank shuddered violently. 'No, no, I just shook her and she fell sideways. She was so limp and—and cool to the touch. I realized she wasn't breathing. Her heart wasn't moving. I tried her pulse but I knew she was dead.'

The doctor snorted. 'Of course she was dead. She was stabbed to death. In the back of the neck with some sort of sharp implement. She's been murdered.'

Frank's face went whiter than I'd have believed possible.

Then he gave a strangled groan and rushed headlong from the room. The toilet door slammed behind him.

Dr Edgely shook his head. 'A bad case of nerves. I'll see what I can do. Someone call the police. And you'd all better stay here until they arrive. They'll want as many witnesses as they can get.'

Angela had lifted her head at the doctor's pronouncement but hadn't uttered a word. I wondered at her self-control as she said, quite calmly, 'Micky, you know someone—an Inspector, isn't he? Will you call him?'

Fiona pushed a phone towards me in an unseeing way and I began to dial.

Don had made coffee for us all and we sipped its comforting warmth and made awkward, broken conversation, trying not to listen to the police machine going about its efficient business in the garden. Dr Edgely's brisk voice sounded on the verandah outside the office door.

'I'll push off, then. You know where my surgery is if I can help. Can't offer any suggestions, anyway. Good luck to you.' He was answered indistinctly by the gloomy voice of Dr Thengalis, the government Medical Officer who'd arrived minutes before the police.

The door opened abruptly and Dr Edgely looked in.

'I'm on my way, John. These blokes—' he gestured outside—'have got it all under control.' He gave Frank Young a sharp, professional stare. 'You all right now?'

Frank looked embarrassed. 'Yes, yes, thanks, Doctor. I'll be fine.'

'You look bloody,' Edgely informed him bluntly. 'Get home as soon as you can, have a stiff drink of whatever you fancy and go to bed.' He glanced at the rest of us, a flicker of interest in his eyes. 'That goes for all of you. Good night.' And he was gone, snapping the door to behind him.

Angela broke a long silence. 'Why did he look at us like that?'

Thinks one of us is a murderer, I said to myself. Probably never met one before.

As if she had caught the unspoken words Angela shivered and relapsed into her own private thoughts, gazing vacantly at the large window which overlooked the now brightly floodlit terraces below. From the office we could see only the tree-tops, a maze of spider webs glistening in the bright police light. For anything more we'd have had to go to the window and look directly down and no one was showing that much curiosity.

The murmur of voices and click of a camera made an oddly unreal background and every now and then a flash illuminated the window.

'How much longer will they be?' Gwen Bright burst out. She'd finally stopped crying and had carefully made up her face again. Surprisingly, she showed little effect from her prolonged bout of tears. Most women of my acquaintance don't get off so lightly. As soon as she'd spoken she gave a quick look at a silent figure standing by the door and bit her lip. At that moment the door opened again and a tall, red-haired man stood silhouetted against the light beyond. The watcher by the door drew himself to attention.

'Thanks, Constable.' Inspector Reeves took him aside and after a brief conversation the young man who had been assigned to the office since the police arrived slipped out.

David Reeves smiled ruefully at me and then extended it to the rest of the room.

'I'm sorry, ladies and gentlemen. I know you're fed up with waiting and we'll get to you as quickly as possible. My sergeants will be here in a moment to look after you, then we'll take your statements and let you get off home, which I'm sure you'll be very glad to do.'

There was a knock at the door and the constable appeared again and stood waiting.

'We've got some chairs around the shop upstairs,' David continued, 'and we'll ask you to wait there until you're called.' He cast another swift look around the office. 'Mr Riley, I'd like to use this room, if that's not a problem.'

'No, go ahead.' John started nervously. He looked all in. He'd met the police when they'd arrived, given them a brief outline of the events of the evening and then rejoined us for the interminable wait.

'Good. Then if you'd all like to move upstairs,' David suggested gently and we gathered ourselves.

'Not you, Micky,' David recalled me. 'I'll talk to you first. Take the others up, Constable.'

CHAPTER 12

David Reeves motioned me to a chair and sat on the corner of John Riley's desk, toying idly with a bronze paper knife. I suddenly remembered Maddy was stabbed in the neck and shuddered.

'It wasn't a knife.' David saw my fixed gaze and sensed my thoughts. 'Some sort of sharp implement, probably round, about a centimetre across, according to Dr Thengalis. We've searched the yard—not a sign of anything like a murder weapon but we're still trying. Anyone could have taken it with them, of course.' He put down the knife and looked me over. 'I gather this isn't a normal feature of your book launches? It's just that you do have a way of being around trouble.'

'Oh, come on, David,' I protested. 'Once or twice . . .' His eyebrows rose slowly. 'Well, perhaps more.'

'Definitely more. Do you know all these people?' He glanced at a paper he'd placed on the desk. The list of guests who'd RSVP'd.

'Not all. Anyone can come, of course. The Rileys have an invitation list as does Lewis and Wilde, my publishers, and I add my list of friends. Those people receive personal invitations. Then there are flyers printed to advertise the launch. They're put on the counter upstairs. Anyone can come by simply ringing and saying so. Some don't even bother to do that—just turn up.'

'It's quite a list.' David ran his eye down the some hundred plus names. 'How many people were here tonight, roughly?'

'I'd say a hundred and twenty, perhaps a few more. It's pretty hard to judge from the gazebo. The Rileys would have a better idea.'

The door opened and a handsome young man, casual in blue denim jeans and a matching jacket, entered and smiled at me. I shook his outstretched hand. Sergeant Harry Andrews was neither as young nor as casual as he appeared but his dark good looks proved extremely useful, according to his Inspector, for interviewing recalcitrant young women.

'Ah, good!' Reeves looked up. 'Has the WPC arrived yet?'

Andrews nodded. 'Constable Shaw.'

'Right. Bring her in with you when I give you a call. You've got a list of these people? I'll just finish with Mr Douglas here—' the Sergeant grinned—'then you can bring the girl in, Miss Grey. We'll do her first so the poor child can go home.'

I broke in. 'She'll be going to Tony and Becky Ridgeway's. She can't go to her own home. Becky will look after her until we can arrange something.'

'We?' Reeves looked quickly from under his bushy red brows. 'A protégée of yours?'

'Sort of. A very dear friend.'

'In that case we'd better take the Ridgeways after Miss Grey and clear them all off.' Andrews left the room and David sat opposite me and laid out various papers and his notebook on the desk between us. He looked up at me pensively. 'I want your account first. From what I gather you were in a unique position to observe the crowd, looking up at them as you were.'

'I couldn't see everything, not properly,' I protested. 'It was pretty dark by then.' I meant Maddy.

'By when?' David gave me a quizzical look.

'By—hell! When was she killed, anyway?'

'Impossible to give an exact time. We'll try to narrow it down. Just tell me how you saw things.'

I frowned, marshalling my thoughts. I'd been over and over the sequence of events in my mind, trying to get straight all the comings and goings that had distracted me throughout the launch, working out who could have gone near Maddy, then realizing I didn't know if I wanted to know.

'I see Madeline Grey was launching your book,' David remarked. 'What was she doing at the back of the garden?'

I told him the whole story. He listened attentively and made notes, stopping me only to clarify a point here, ask a question there.

'From what you've told me,' he said drily as I wound to a tired halt, 'all the people upstairs had a grudge against the deceased and benefit by her death in some way.'

'Not all,' I countered quickly. 'Becky wasn't on Maddy's hate list, neither was Frank Young, and I doubt if Karen Blair bothered her, apart from Angela's obvious crush on her.' I suddenly remembered it was Karen who'd man-handled Maddy at the studio and faltered, but continued as confidently as I could. 'Gwen Bright was pretty sure Maddy would come around. She always did, you know. I thought it would probably all blow over in a few days. She'd create these huge rows, insult everyone, come to her senses within a week, realize the damage she'd done to herself and make amends. Expensive boxes of chocolates from Chocs, little bunches of flowers, other special gifts, and she'd have them all back around her. She seemed to know exactly how far to go with anyone and she'd stop just in time.'

'Not this time,' David said quietly. 'This time she went too far with someone.'

He flipped back through his notebook. 'I want to check those times again. Riley opened the evening just after six —six-five, in fact. Pretty good, considering the high drama going on. In the meantime Rebecca Ridgeway, better known as Rebecca Rowland, was asked to take Mrs Grey's place and she began to speak—when? Six-ten?'

'John only took a few minutes; three or four at the most.'

'Right. Mrs Ridgeway spoke for five minutes, so it was just before six-fifteen when you took the microphone. Some minutes later you noticed Mrs Grey coming down the stairs from the office.'

'It was six-twenty-five,' I said. 'I know because I looked at my watch to see if it was time to wind up. I wanted to avoid trouble.'

'I'm not surprised,' David murmured. 'Go on.'

'I saw her bump into the journalist, Jessica Savage. I hoped Jessica might distract her but she just moved aside. She knew the state Maddy was in, though. Probably planning a nice juicy story for her column. She'd been hanging around the back stairs—hoping to catch Maddy making a fool of herself, I suppose.'

'You saw Miss Savage earlier?'

I shrugged. 'She's pretty striking. Hard to miss. I was looking up when Becky started her bit and noticed Jess on the stairs under the light. You get a good view from there, over all the heads, and Jessica's not very tall. I thought then she must have been lying in wait for a scandal. She wasn't there a few minutes later, though, so she must have come into the garden. After that, she was on the verandah.'

'When did you see her on the verandah?'

I suddenly remembered the incident which had made me look up and reddened.

'Ah, oh—just a few minutes before Maddy came down, I think. Really, David, I'm not sure.'

He gave me a disbelieving look and I inwardly cursed my face for its giveaway flush.

'You'd better tell me, you know. You've blown it, any-how. Something happened, I gather.'

I swallowed. 'I just don't want to—to give any false impressions,' I blurted out.

'I think we can decide for ourselves what impressions, if any, we arrive at,' David said impatiently. 'We're not exactly known for jumping to wrong conclusions. Come on, Micky. Get on with it.'

'I heard a door close,' I said reluctantly. 'I thought: Oh horrors, here she comes, and I looked up. Fiona Riley had come out of the office. She ran back up to the shop and I noticed Jessica on the verandah. It must have been just before six-twenty-five. She was back on the stairs when Maddy came out and she followed her down—to get as much as she could out of it, of course.'

David looked at me for a moment, then picked out the one detail I hoped I'd slipped past him.

'Miss Riley must have closed the door pretty sharply for you to hear it in the gazebo. What was she doing in the office?'

'I didn't ask her,' I said stiffly. 'She probably looked in to see if Maddy was OK.'

'And slammed the door on the way out? All right, we'll leave it at that. I expect Miss Savage saw what happened.'

I remembered the way Jessica had watched the distressed Fiona run up the stairs into the building and felt distinctly annoyed. Jessica would put all sorts of interpretations on what was probably a perfectly innocent event. I said noth-ing. David waited.

'No?' he said at last and I could see the sudden humour lurking in his eyes. 'Then we'll move on. Now, Mr Ridge-way headed Mrs Grey off and took her to the seat at the back of the garden?'

'Yes, but I couldn't see Maddy there. The chairs were

under some tree ferns. It was very dark. In a minute or so
Tony came back into the light and went over to the table.
He got a drink and went back to Maddy.'

'Ah yes, it was Mr Ridgeway who claimed to have killed
the lady.'

'He didn't know she was stabbed. He thought she'd
died of the drink and sleeping tablets. A heart attack or
something.'

'So Dr Edgely said. Now we come to the crucial moments. Between now—we've arrived at six-twenty-five—
and eight pm, someone went into the shadows and
despatched Madeline Grey. Think carefully, Micky. Who
did you notice around that area?'

My mind once again uncomfortably surveyed the scene.
'Well,' I said slowly, 'Jessica had moved down further. I
was taking questions from the audience so I was looking up
into the crowd then. She was standing on the bottom step,
just above Frank Young. He was talking with Gillian Fry,
the author.'

'Did you see them there earlier?'

'I noticed Gillian coming down the stairs just as I took
the mike. People were using the pause to get another drink
or a snack. Then they generally moved forward again so
there were only a few at the back. Frank had been there
earlier. He'd seemed concerned about Maddy—said he
pitied her. I think he must have been keeping an eye out
for her.'

'Dr Edgely informed us Mr Young was in a state of shock
and distress and became ill when told Mrs Grey had been
stabbed. The doctor gave him a couple of tablets to settle
his stomach. Was Mr Young a particular friend of Mrs
Grey?'

'I don't think so. I met him at one of her parties but I
didn't think he paid her special attention. He left early to
go home to his wife. I got the impression he didn't actually
like Maddy much.'

'I see.' David made a note. 'Go on.'

'Fiona came back down about then to help serve. People usually stay and chat afterwards. Don Riley was there, of course, at the table on the left of the stairs as you look up from the gazebo. He was pouring drinks and looking after the food.'

'Did he leave the table at all?'

'Yes, to take a tray around or to go back up to the kitchen for supplies.'

'Right. Anyone else around the area?'

'I don't know. I'd started signing books again and talking with people. I did notice Angela run up the stairs to the office. She couldn't have realized Maddy had come down. Everybody started to drift up to the back of the garden but Maddy was in the dark corner at the far right, looking up from the gazebo again, and no one went near her that I could see. They wouldn't have known she was there.' I stopped suddenly. David looked at me keenly.

'Yes? Someone did go over to her?'

'I was jumpy. I couldn't help checking that it was still all quiet up the back. Bobby West was by the drinks table. Then he went over to that corner. I was relieved to see Tony and Becky by the stairs as well. I thought: If she comes out, West and the Ridgeways will hold on to her.'

'Sounds like a happy gathering,' David remarked.

'It was bloody,' I said feelingly. 'Never again!' Then I realized what I'd said and shut up, embarrassed.

'Can you pinpoint the time that Mr West went over to Mrs Grey?'

'God, no! Not long after Angela ran up to the office. Five minutes, perhaps? It wasn't long after that I was able to move and I went up the garden and mingled. Bobby was signing autographs. Angela was sitting on a bench about half way up, Frank was surrounded by women and I saw Gillian Fry signing a book. Fiona brought me a drink and something to eat and told me Maddy was unconscious. I moved up to the back with Gwen Bright, Maddy's agent, and the Rileys were cleaning up. There were still twenty or so people around the top terrace but I didn't see anyone close to Maddy's corner. I thanked the Ridgeways for their sterling effort and we all chatted. In the end it was just the people upstairs. Angela suggested we get Maddy home and Frank went to wake her up. He came back looking sick and said she was dead. Tony was stunned and tried to push Frank aside and said he must have killed her. John Riley took over, confirmed she was dead, took us into the office and sent Don for Dr Edgely. That's all, David.'

CHAPTER 13

David Reeves looked through his notes then up at me.

'Pretty daring thing to do,' he said thoughtfully, 'sur-rounded by people. Anyone might have seen the murderer go over to Mrs Grey although he—or she—was masked by the shadows. Anyone who knew the deceased was there could have gone to her, bent over her solicitously, pretended to talk to her—and struck her. If she was unconscious with the drink and sleeping pills, what could be easier?'

'But who?' I asked hoarsely. 'I can't believe it was anyone I saw. Bobby? Tony?'

'We'll get the truth,' David said gently. 'Out of a hundred and twenty people, someone knows who did it—probably without knowing they know.' He raised his voice and called and the door opened promptly. Sergeant Andrews came in accompanied by a uniformed policewoman. She was in her early thirties and looked friendly and competent. Harry set her a chair in a corner and she settled herself and took out a notebook.

'Constable Shaw.' David smiled at her. 'The Sergeant has explained the situation?'

'Yes, sir.'

'Good. Harry, I want you here with me. You can bring Miss Grey down.'

I stirred. 'David, would you mind if I stayed? Angie's only fourteen. She's known me all her life. It might be less of an ordeal if she had a friend with her.'

David smiled slightly. 'Well, so far you're the only one I'm pretty sure can't have done for her mother. You've a hundred and twenty witnesses for most of the evening and I gather you were never alone. All right, Micky, you might be useful at that, if you'd like to sit in for a while. I believe these TV people can be very temperamental. That's fifty per cent temper and fifty per cent mental,' he added unexpectedly and his eyes twinkled. 'But, for God's sake, don't interrupt.'

Andrews pulled up another chair, grinning at my protests. David said, 'A private word, Harry,' and walked with him to the door. I heard him say, 'Tell Brian,' but the rest was too low for me to hear. Harry nodded once or twice, gave a soft whistle of surprise and went out. David didn't satisfy my curiosity and the Sergeant was back almost immediately and ushered Angela into the room. She looked calm and more self-possessed than I'd have been in her place but her face was pale and she stumbled slightly. I went to meet her and brought her across to the second chair. She sat gracefully, the only sign of nerves in the fingers which clutched her bag.

'Miss Grey.' The Inspector smiled kindly at her. 'I'm sorry to have kept you. May I offer my condolences? I realize how you must be feeling and we'll get this over as quickly as possible so you can leave.'

'Thank you.' Angela's voice was steady. 'I'm all right.'

'Do you object to Mr Douglas being present? He thought it might help.'

'Micky?' Angela looked surprised. 'Of course not. I can't tell you anything, anyway. I was half way down, closer to the front, on one of the benches. I didn't see anything behind me. I didn't see who—who . . .' She broke off uncertainly.

'Then we'll just quickly run through the events as you remember them. Constable Shaw here will take it down in shorthand and we'll ask you to come in to police headquarters tomorrow and sign the statement when it's typed up, OK?'

'Fine.' Her fingers relaxed a little.

Angela's statement was brief. She gave the facts clearly in a rather wooden voice, still showing no trace of emotion. My heart went out to her. She'd had to shut off her feelings so many times in her young life. She said that Maddy had been angry all day but not losing her temper as she usually did. 'It was worse. Sort of all shut up inside her.' She'd been drinking but didn't seem too bad. Angela thought, from her experience, her mother was quite capable of pulling herself together and launching the book.

'Micky sent me downstairs with Bobby, Bobby West, to get a drink. I thought Mum would be fine. I didn't know she'd taken a bad turn until she didn't come down with Micky and Mr Riley and then Tony came to ask Becky if she'd do the launch. I wanted to go up to Mum but Tony said not to draw attention to her and she was all right. As soon as the launch was over I ran up to the office to make sure she was still OK and she'd gone. I went back down and asked Tony what had happened. I thought she might have gone home in a temper or been sleeping in the car outside.'

'What did you do when Mr Ridgeway told you she'd come into the garden?'

'I went to see her. I saw Bobby West come out from the corner where she was and I went over to her.' She looked at David calmly. 'She was asleep. I thought it would be best to let her stay until the people had all gone. Not embarrass her by waking her up.'

'Miss Grey, you're sure she was asleep?'

'Of course,' Angela said shortly. 'If you want the full details, she was asleep and her mouth was open and she was snoring—quite loudly, in fact. I didn't want the others to see her like that.' Her shoulders suddenly sagged and she covered her face with her hands.

I leaned over and touched her arm. 'It's all right, Angel.' Then I thought: What a bloody stupid thing to say to a child whose mother had just been murdered.

David mimed taking a drink and jerked his head towards the kitchen. Harry got up quickly and returned in a minute with a glass of water which he gave to Angela. She took a sip, then looked quietly at David.

'I went back to Bobby but it didn't take long before he got surrounded and started signing autographs. I waited for him to finish, then we joined the Ridgeways and Gwen Bright and Frank and Micky. I asked Tony if Mum was OK and he said she was still asleep. Then Frank went to wake her up and Tony said I should let Bobby take me home and he and Becky would look after Mum.'

'But you didn't want to do that?' David asked.

'I don't run out on people when they're in trouble.' Angie sounded scornful. 'I'm all Mum's got. I could cope.'

David murmured something non-committal. Angela had no more to offer but her story tallied pretty exactly with what I'd seen. The Inspector nodded towards the policewoman and she came over to Angela and smiled at her.

'I'm going to ask you something now,' David said calmly. 'I hope you won't let it upset you. It's routine, I'm afraid. I'll be asking everyone.' He threw me a warning look. 'I want you to go to the Ladies with Constable Shaw and let her give you a quick search. It's not a strip or anything like that. And she'll look through your bag.'

I stifled a protest and Angela looked thoughtfully at me. 'I don't mind, Micky. Come on, then, Constable.'

'What on *earth*!' I burst out as the door to the toilet area closed behind them.

'I told you not to interrupt,' David said sternly, and Harry had a private smile.

'Bugger that!' I retorted indignantly. 'Why in the name of—hell!' The penny dropped with a mind-numbing jolt. 'The murder weapon.'

'It would help if we found it, you know.' David was gently ironic.

'Well, you won't find it in Angela's bag!' I said crossly.

Angela returned within minutes. I was relieved to see she was still looking composed and even had a touch of colour back in her face. David thanked her and Andrews escorted her out.

There was a tap on the door and Sergeant Hobbs looked in. He gave me a sympathetic smile and advanced into the room at a nod from his chief. His sober grey suit and short grizzled hair were distinctly dishevelled. He caught a glimpse of his reflection on the window and surveyed himself ruefully, smoothing down his hair, then turned back to me.

'Well, it's very nice to see you again, Mr Douglas, although not in very happy circumstances for you.'

I shook his hand. 'Hello, Sergeant. No, pretty distressing for everyone.'

'Any luck, Brian?' David asked.

'No, sir, not yet. Not in the bins. Young Mr Riley has cleared everything up and thrown all the rubbish away so there was a bit to go through. No sign of anything suspicious. Just food scraps, plastic cups, paper plates, used wine casks, that sort of thing. We'll continue outside, then I'll start on the kitchen and the toilets.'

'Do that, Brian. And when you've finished there, I notice there's another office.' He pointed across the room. Sergeant Hobbs opened the adjoining door to reveal a clutter of packaging materials, boxes full of books, empty cartons

stacked against the wall and a small desk piled high with
books, manilla folders and invoices. More piles of books
fought for space on the floor.

'Courage, Sergeant! It may not come to that.' Reeves had
caught the fleeting grimace crossing Hobbs's face.

'Never mind, sir, lucky it's still quite early. I'll get on
with it, then.' He went out, passing Sergeant Andrews in
the doorway.

'Mrs Ridgeway?' Reeves inquired.

'Waiting outside, sir.'

'Bring her in, Harry. Let's get through this lot before the
night gets any older.'

CHAPTER 14

Rebecca Ridgeway met the Inspector's admiring gaze with
a friendly smile and settled herself in the chair vacated by
Angela.

'I hope this won't take long, Inspector, I need to get that
poor girl home.'

'We'll be as quick as we can, Mrs Ridgeway. We just
need an account of the events of this evening as you remember them.'

Becky shrugged. 'I assume you mean after we arrived.
Before that we'd picked up Maddy and Angela as arranged,
only to find—well, I'm sure you've heard the story.'

'Why did you collect the Greys? Was that a normal thing
to do?'

A shadow of annoyance crossed her lovely face. 'Unfortunately, it was becoming a necessity. Maddy has been—
unpredictable, to say the least. Tony, my husband, Inspector, has realized for some time that if it's a studio matter,
publicity affair or like this evening, it's advisable to pick
Maddy up early, just in case she needs—well—help to pull

herself together, I'm sorry to say—and to make sure she does arrive on time and in a fit state.'

'Was there any reason to think she needed to be checked up on tonight?'

'Again, unfortunately, yes. Tony dropped by Maddy's last night and found her in a very disturbed state. She wanted to sack Bobby West from *Kids' World*. She gave no reason but was adamant that he had to go. Tony managed to calm her down by telling her he'd consider it. He never meant to. Maddy takes these odd sets against people and then it all dies down again. Probably in a day or two she'd have been all over Bobby like a rash. There was an incident at the studio—the Saturday before last, I think it was. Maddy had been unfit for work for a few days and Bobby and the rest of the team were pre-taping various segments to get ahead. Maddy turned up, very abusive, and accused Bobby and Tony of trying to take over the show behind her back. She'd settled down by the following Monday and Bobby was her golden boy again. So Tony thought this was a similar situation.'

'Was the relationship between Mr West and Mrs Grey usually amicable?'

Becky pulled a face. 'Well, it's no secret, Inspector. Four years ago they were lovers. Poor Bobby didn't have a chance, of course. Maddy is—was—rather a rapacious woman. She took one look at Bobby and ate him up. It was very flattering to him to walk off with the goddess under the noses of all her other worshippers. Of course, for her part, she was just using him. Like all her victims, he was dazzled, he adored her, couldn't see how destructive she was, although, heaven knows, I tried to open his eyes. Then she dropped him without compunction. Took up with someone else. I never heard who it was. Bobby went around looking like a sick, abandoned puppy for weeks, but he got over it. Then it was back to a normal working relationship, apparently no hard feelings.'

'And how long ago did this personal relationship end?'

'Two years?' Becky threw me an interrogative look and I nodded.

'Yes, easily.'

She gave a little amused snort. 'You're not thinking Bobby went mad and took a knife to Maddy in a fit of jealousy or something, I hope? He was relieved to be out of it, believe me.'

'And there was no animosity between them in spite of her accusations last week that he was trying to take over her show?'

'Oh, that!' Becky made a dismissive gesture. 'Forget it, Inspector, it was a storm in a teacup. She's been fine all week.'

'So you have no idea what triggered her sacking of Mr West earlier today?'

'She didn't need an excuse to be bloody-minded. She could easily have sacked him under any pretext, just to show him she had control, then repent and take him back again, it's all a game. I honestly don't think she sees—saw —the damage she did to people. Well, she played her game once to often, it seems.'

Reeves was watching her shrewdly. 'You didn't like Mrs Grey?'

'I loathed her,' Becky said frankly. 'She made Tony's life hell. In the early days, when Tony first teamed up with Morgan, Maddy was always making excuses to get him around to her place, throwing tantrums, trying to manipulate him. She didn't like me, of course, because I was married to Tony and she couldn't get him away from me—and she tried very hard, Inspector. She saw all men as her preserve. Good-looking ones, anyway. Wives were a mere detail that didn't bother her. Tony was the only one who didn't get sucked in. However—' she smiled suddenly— 'don't get excited, Inspector. I've loathed her for years. Just habit. A very passive habit. I promise you I didn't kill her

—didn't even want her dead, particularly. She was good for the show. *Kids' World* saved Channel 6 in the early days and gave Tony his big break. Anyway, I can prove it wasn't me,' she said seriously. 'I was surrounded by witnesses all night, so I couldn't have done it.'

A glimmer of amusement flickered in David's eyes but his voice retained its professional tone.

'Perhaps you'd go over your movements—for the record.'

'Of course. I arrived with my husband, Maddy, Angela and Gwen Bright. We met Bobby at the door. He'd just arrived in that lovely sports car of his. He was suitably horrified to hear of Maddy's condition and seemed to blame himself, though heaven knows why. Bobby took Angela in and Tony went to tell Micky the bad news. He came back with John Riley and we managed to steer Maddy through the shop without anyone noticing, although we bumped into Gillian Fry and she heard us talking and that awful Savage woman was browsing through the books, so I'm sure she knew what was going on. She's been laying into Maddy for years for filching Morgan from her. We got Maddy into the office—she really wasn't too bad, and started pouring Barbara's coffee into her. I went out to do my bit with the crowd and let Micky know all wasn't lost. I kept a pretty good eye on the verandah, of course, and saw John bringing Micky down. By that time I'd joined Angela and Bobby and we grabbed a seat. Next thing Tony appeared and asked me to take Maddy's place, which I was delighted to do.' She smiled at me. 'Poor Micky had been through quite enough. I finished my talk and sat with John Riley at the back of the gazebo—notice, Inspector, in full view of the public—until Micky finished and I can tell you exactly when that was. It was seven o'clock precisely. I looked at my watch.'

'Then what did you do, Mrs Ridgeway?'

'I went and mingled. Did my duty. Tony found me and got me a drink, thank goodness, and we stayed together talking to people until the end, when Angela gave Tony the nod to wake up her mum and Frank nipped in first and made his rather sickening announcement.'

'You found it sickening?'

'I found it extremely disturbing.' She met his look and said simply, 'Violence always disturbs me and the ultimate violence must be to take another's life. I don't think Maddy deserved that. To die like that—drunk, alone, with all her fears, hated by so many people. It—it was indecent. I felt terribly sorry for Angela. She's always tried to shield her mother and out of common decency I think we should try to silence any scandal. Murder won't help.'

Reeves shook his head gravely. 'No, Mrs Ridgeway, murder won't help, although we'll be as discreet as we can.'

'Well, just remember the number of people who've suffered for Maddy and will be doubly hurt if a half of this comes out.' She smiled at him. 'You seem like a very nice man, Inspector. I expect you'll see us right.'

'Thank you,' David said gravely. 'I'd like you to cast your mind back and tell me what you observed happening while you were in the gazebo. Who went up and down the stairs, who was at the back of the garden, that sort of thing.'

'Oh, help!' She narrowed her eyes, looking back over the evening. 'Well, now, I did see Gillian Fry on the stairs—half way down—just as Micky started his talk. Angela had pointed her out earlier. She thought Miss Fry was wonderful. She said Maddy couldn't stand her. Naturally, Maddy hated anyone Angela admired. She wanted to be Angela's only idol. Oh dear, that was very catty, but it's true, unhappily. After that I was watching Micky and listening to what he had to say. He was very good, lots of humour. Oh yes, of course, Fiona Riley came out of the office looking like thunder—yes, I could see her clearly in the light. She slammed the door, made me look up. Well, I was rather expecting someone else. Fiona was crying her eyes out. She ran up to the shop. There was someone else—yes, the

Savage woman was hanging around. That was at about
six-twenty-five because just before, John had whispered to
me that it was going well and I looked at my watch to see
what the time was. I'd make an excellent witness.' She
looked slightly embarrassed. 'Oh! Sorry, I am a witness.
Then I remember Micky suddenly looked like a rabbit
caught in a car's headlights—sorry, Micky, but you looked
quite glazed—and he stumbled over his words. I thought
he'd dried up unexpectedly although it didn't seem like
him. I wasn't watching the back at the time or I'd have
known why he froze. I was taken by some children at the
front. Micky finished at six-forty-five and took questions
from the audience. A cute little boy came down and asked
him if Winifred was real, and I did notice Jessica Savage
listening to everything Frank Young and Gillian Fry were
saying, the snoop. And I saw Fiona Riley come down the
stairs. Of course, later Tony told me what happened but I
only caught part of it because he was whispering. I saw
Gwen Bright earlier. I remembered that when I finally
grasped that Maddy was under the tree ferns in the far
corner, because I'd seen Gwen go over there and vaguely
wondered why, then later thought: Oh, that's why.'

'When was that?' Reeves cut in.

'You mean Gwen? Let me see, perhaps five minutes after
I'd checked the time—say six-thirtyish. Thereabouts, anyway. I looked up and Tony was standing at the back watching us and Gwen was sort of sidling in a very odd way
towards the far right-hand corner of the terrace. She'd been
standing by the drinks table. Mind you, Gwen's been a
little strange all week. Maddy told her she was dumping
her and Gwen went around like Cassandra, if that's the
lady I mean, for days, then started making excuses for
Maddy and doing everything to get back in her good books.
You'd think she'd have counted her blessings, but not her!
Poor woman blamed herself. Can you imagine? Said she'd
let Maddy down. So stupid. Maddy was like a very

powerful drug, Inspector, in case you haven't realized. For those afflicted by her she was very hard to give up. Gwen's probably blaming herself for Maddy's death right now.'

'Did you see Miss Bright return?'

'No, just noted that she looked odd and said, "Par for the course", and forgot it. I was more interested in Micky.'

'Hmmm!' David smiled at her. 'Nothing more to tell me?'

'Not a thing. Sorry, Inspector. I'd love to be able to say, "I saw the murderer, weapon held aloft, sneak into the shrubbery . . ."' She stopped and gave a sudden gasp. 'No, I wouldn't. It occurs to me that, whoever it is, I probably know him or her rather well and, while I might sympathize with their motive, I—I really can't condone murder. That's all I can tell you, Inspector. Now, let me get back to Angela, please.'

CHAPTER 15

Becky received the suggestion that she be searched with an amused look. As with Angela it didn't take long and she farewelled me with a hug.

'I'm so sorry about all this, Micky. It's rotten for you.'

Tony Ridgeway was ushered in to make his statement. There'd been nothing said between Reeves and Andrews in the intervals between what I now recognized distastefully as the suspects, so I had no idea what was going through their minds. All I knew was there was no way Angela or Becky could have been guilty.

'Mind if I smoke?' Tony sat back and lit a cigarette. Reeves pushed an ashtray towards him.

'Thanks. Well, Inspector, ask me whatever you like. I'm anxious to get this over quickly. It's caused me no end of a headache. I've got a show to get together. Probably be up all night making arrangements. Thank God we've got a

lot pre-taped, but this'll stuff the schedule.' He slapped the
arm of his chair. 'What a bloody turn of events.'

Reeves went through the preliminaries once again, then
asked about the producer's visit to Maddy the previous
night.

'Just had a hunch.' Tony shook his head. 'I promised
Micky I'd keep an eye on her and make sure she was OK
for the launch. Very well behaved all week, Maddy was,
but—simmering under the surface, you know? Had a spat
with Gwenny, Tuesday, but still too calm for Maddy. Well,
I learnt a long time ago that it wasn't smart to let her
simmer too long. I'm a great believer in talking things
through, working it out. I could always handle Maddy. So
I just dropped in, casual, to see if she needed to let off
steam. A producer's a kind of psychiatrist, father figure,
counsellor, you name it, Inspector, I'll do it to keep my
people happy. They want to talk, I'll listen.'

'You felt Mrs Grey wanted to talk?'

'I know Maddy better than most. Started with her husband, Morgan Grey, back in 'seventy-six. Maddy was great
in those days. A stunner, of course, just twenty-one, everything going for her, a major star already. She had the knack.
Not the head for it, which caused all the trouble, but the
knack. And the looks! Blokes all around her from the start.'
Tony ran a hand through his hair and seemed lost for a
moment in past memories. 'Good days, they were, Inspector, good days.'

'Were you one of Mrs Grey's—court, Mr Ridgeway?'

He sat up with a jerk. 'Christ, no! I was married to Becky
and she was good enough for me. I wasn't about to lose my
head over Madeline Grey. Anyway, Morgan was a good
mate. I don't say she didn't try,' Tony added, 'but I could
handle that one.'

I frowned. There'd been just a touch of complacency in
his voice—but, then, perhaps he had the right to feel smug.
There weren't many who could say they'd turned down

Maddy Grey—and back then she'd been almost irresistible.

'Tell me about Sunday night. How did you find Mrs Grey?'

'Well, look, you had to know her. On the surface she was very calm. "Darling, I've been thinking over a few things," she said. Nothing in that, she called everybody "darling". I said, "What sort of things," and she trotted out this plan. She'd worked it all out. She felt Bobby'd have more of a career opportunity out of *Kids' World*. Won a Logie for Best New Talent when he started, you know. She thought she was holding him back. She'd like to see him go down south and get into some series or other, she could wangle it for him, she reckoned. Then she started on Angela. It wasn't good for the kid to be hanging around the studios. It was giving her all sorts of ideas, she wasn't cut out for show business. She'd been looking up boarding-schools. Had a plan to send Angie away to a good girls' school in the country—get her back to a normal life, she said. She told me she knew she'd put Angie through a lot with the drinking and the kid deserved a break. Talked about sending her to Europe in the school holidays.'

'That sounds reasonable,' David murmured.

'Oh yeah? A mother doing her duty? Forget it, Inspector. Maddy didn't have a motherly bone in her body. Catch her worrying about the kid's best interests. Maddy was Maddy's top priority. And let me tell you, she wouldn't be doing young Bobby a favour without a mighty good reason.' He leaned forward and stubbed out his cigarette.

'And what was her reason?'

'Well! You tell me. I couldn't get her to open up. Maybe she was getting at me for encouraging Angie. I reckoned she'd be a winner in a small part in the show, but Maddy wouldn't hear of it. Jealous as a cat. She might have been letting me know she was in control. Said I should let Bobby go right now. Pigs—sorry, Inspector. I told her I'd think about it. She'd have got it all out of her system, you know.

Bobby's great in the show. He doesn't want to leave and he's got a big following. I wasn't going to dump him. But when I left her, she was OK, I can tell you. She'd said her piece, played whatever game she had in mind and thought I was going along with it. So, you tell me! What set her off? I don't know. One thing I do know, though, she was expecting Gwenny Bright. If anything happened on Sunday night, Gwenny'd know. You ask her.'

'We'll do that, Mr Ridgeway. Now, let's come to to-night's events. You picked the Greys up and found Mrs Grey intoxicated?'

'Oh, I knew what condition she'd be in. I'd had her and her solicitor and God knows who else on the phone all day. She was mad as a hornet and taking it out on everyone. She'd done an illegal deal with Gabrielle Mentos at Channel 8, sacked Bobby from the show, dropped the Rileys right in it—and had a hell of a row with Gwenny, I gather.'

'And yet Miss Bright was apparently there tonight at the Greys' house.'

'It was pathetic,' Tony said shortly. 'Poor little woman, hanging about, practically fawning at Maddy's feet. Oh, she knew how to get around Maddy. And Maddy needed Gwen, we all knew that. No other agent would take her on, behaving as she did, although she liked to kid herself she was in demand. Gwen had been with her from the start and was more like a mother than an agent. Adored Maddy, put up with her moods. Dropping Gwen would have been a fatal error.'

'So you brought the Greys and Miss Bright to the book-shop.'

'Yes, Maddy wasn't too bad. I should have been more sussy, though. She was almost too rational. I knew she'd been drinking heavily but it didn't show much. That's got to be a bad sign, but I was just relieved she could still do the job. We got her in, Barbara Riley and I got coffee into her, she was very apologetic and pulled herself around—

then it all came unstuck. I'd been left with her to make sure she did the job and out of the blue she started shaking and crying and said she couldn't do it. Her nerves just snapped. She was a mess. I couldn't reason with her and I've seen her nervy hundreds of times before a public do. But this time! Well, I'd have had to carry her down, Inspector, that's God's truth, and a fine book launch that would have been. So I left her. What could I do?'

'In fact, until then, you had thought the nerves were quite normal for her and she was sober enough to launch the book?'

'That's right.' Ridgeway lit another cigarette and narrowed his eyes against the smoke.

'You didn't give her any more alcohol? Perhaps a drink to calm her nerves?'

'Christ!' He stared at the Inspector. 'You'd be joking. No one in their right mind would have fed her any more.'

'But later you admitted to having given her a glass of wine—laced with sleeping tablets?'

He looked sheepish. 'Well, by then it was a bit late, wasn't it? She was bent on wrecking the launch. Felt guilty and wanted to go down and make it up to Micky. I couldn't talk her out of it. So I said she should just sit for a minute and catch her breath and I got her a drink. I couldn't knock her out and carry her back up the stairs. All I was thinking was, shut her up for now, and I swore then and there to get her into a clinic. The whole drinking thing had gone too far and I wanted her straightened out.'

'Are you in the habit of carrying sleeping pills?'

'Ah! Look, Inspector, Micky'll back me up here. Maddy'd get drunk, right? Then she'd make a scene and exhaust herself. Then she'd lie awake all night in a panic wondering what she'd done. I started to carry the pills around a few years ago. I'd get her home or on to a sofa somewhere, give her a couple of tablets, she'd sleep it off and wake up like a lamb all ready to make amends. There wasn't any harm in it. If she didn't sleep and just lay there all night, worn out and her mind racing, she'd be a wreck in the morning.'

'I see. So you persuaded her to go with you to a chair under the tree ferns.'

'The darkest spot I could find, yes.'

'Then you fetched her a drink and dissolved the pills in it.'

'And stood by her until she'd drunk it. She started talking, very fast, about how she'd make it all up to us, then she dropped off. I made sure she was asleep and left her before anyone noticed.'

'Did you see Miss Bright?'

'Gwenny? No.'

'Apparently she went over to Mrs Grey after you left her.'

Tony gave a slight shrug. 'Well, she had enough sense to keep her mouth shut. I'm glad she just left Maddy to sleep it off.'

'Did you notice anyone else at the back who might have seen you with Mrs Grey and gone to investigate? Or anyone going over to her?'

'No, I was thankful she was asleep and went back to enjoy the rest of the evening. It was a bit of a weight off my mind. I reckoned she'd be OK there until it was all over and at least I was free to have a drink myself and listen to Micky's talk. I gave him a sign so he'd know it was all right.'

'Think back, Mr Ridgeway. Who was around you at the time?'

'You mean, who could have seen me stow Maddy away and decided to shut her up permanently? Well, the two Riley youngsters seemed to be running up and down the stairs a lot. There were various people coming and going. Jessica Savage was hanging around. I was nearly going to give her a serve for upsetting Maddy but what's the use?

You can't stop her. Maddy was about to sue her for libel. I told her it wasn't libel, that Jess knew what she was about too well to expose herself. Anyway, what she printed was the truth.' He gave a little chuckle. 'If I didn't—if I told her once, I told her a dozen times. Why should she mind? It was only sour grapes. You know Morgan Grey was living with Jess before Maddy came on the scene? That's an old story, Inspector. Now Jess gets her claws into Maddy out of habit.'

David brought Tony back to the question in hand.

'Right, sorry. Frank Young was behind me. Can't miss Frank's voice, has all the girls gooey-eyed. He was talking to some tall woman with frizzy hair. She's waiting upstairs, name of Fry. When the Riley girl started helping her brother set up more drinks I figured the whole thing was just about over. Angie came and asked where Maddy was. She'd run up to the office, of course, and was in a tizz. I told her the story and said not to disturb Maddy until everyone had gone. By then Micky was signing books and there were people going home, some milling around the drinks table—and I was doing my bit, waving the flag for Channel 6 with Becky, so I didn't notice if anyone went near Maddy. Apparently someone must have.'

'You didn't feel the need to watch out for Mrs Grey in case she woke up and made more trouble?'

'I told you, I knew she'd sleep for hours if she wasn't disturbed. No one knew where she was. You could barely see her in the dark. All the light was around the stairs and the drinks table. No, I wasn't worried about that.'

'But apparently Mrs Grey was snoring. Couldn't some-one have heard her and gone to investigate?'

'Who says she was snoring?'

'Miss Grey disregarded your advice. She went to see her mother and found her asleep and snoring.'

Tony's eyebrows went up. 'Did she! Well, I'm glad to say I didn't hear anything so she must have stopped pretty

quickly. Oh Christ!' He sat up in horror. 'What if that was
when she was killed? Someone heard her, realized she was
there and stabbed her?'

'It's a possibility, Mr Ridgeway. We're narrowing down
the time of death. Mr West was seen approaching Mrs
Grey, then her daughter found her asleep, so she was alive
just after ten to seven, as close as we can make it.'

'Well, after that I was flat out! Becky was, too. If you
want an alibi, we've got a dozen of Becky's fans to back us
up.'

Reeves smiled slightly. 'Yes, there seems to be no lack of
witnesses. One more thing, Mr Ridgeway. Did Don Riley
serve you with a drink for Mrs Grey?'

'No, he wasn't at the table. I helped myself.'

'I see. Now I'll just take possession of those pills of yours.
For analysis.'

Tony brought a small bottle from his pocket. 'Take them.
It looks like I won't be needing them any more.'

'Presumably not. Would you object to going with Sergeant Andrews and submitting to a search?'

'Why the hell . . . ? No, I wouldn't mind. Anything I can
do to help, Inspector.'

They went out.

'Isn't everyone nice and cooperative?' David remarked
to the ceiling.

CHAPTER 16

David Reeves frowned and wrote rapidly in his notebook.

'We'd better see Mr Young next, Harry. Dr Edgely
warned me he was a bundle of nerves. See if you can rustle
up some coffee. I hope Constable Bates is on the alert up
there.'

Sergeant Andrews grinned. 'He knows the score, sir.'

'I'll be interested to have his report. And check how Brian's getting along—especially with the alcohol.'

Andrews left the room to return minutes later with Frank Young. The newsreader looked exhausted, his eyes dark-shadowed and deep lines etched in his face.

'Sit down, Mr Young.' David gave his soothing smile. 'We won't keep you long. Do you object to Mr Douglas being present while we talk?'

'No, Inspector. It—it's a relief to see a friendly face. Not that I mean . . .' He tailed off uncertainly.

'I understand, it can be a bit of an ordeal. We've got coffee on the way, I'm sure you'll be glad of a cup. Now, I just need your version of the events that took place tonight. We're trying to pinpoint the time of death as accurately as we can, so anything you can tell us will be useful. It's very likely someone has information and probably doesn't even realize.'

'Yes, I see. What can I tell you, Inspector?'

'Why did you attend the launch, Mr Young?'

'Tony Ridgeway wanted us to support Mr Douglas. He circulated a note, mainly to the *Kids' World* staff, to put in an appearance if they could.'

'You're not associated with *Kids' World*, I understand?'

'No, but I know Mr Douglas. I mentioned it to my wife, Jasmine, and she was insistent that I come. Our children are great fans of Micky's books. I was under orders to buy the book for them and have it autographed.'

'Your family wasn't with you?'

'My two are a little young yet and Jasmine is a very quiet person. She doesn't handle large gatherings well. She always avoids celebrity parties, that sort of thing.'

'I see. You read the evening news?'

'I did until recently. Actually, Russell Scott, our weekend and late night newsreader, is on holiday and I suggested to the producers that I take his place.'

'Why was that?'

'To tell you the truth, without seeming conceited, I hope, the ratings have been dropping at those times. I felt I could boost our audience. I—I have a certain following. The producers agreed and made the change.'

'And it suits you? The odd hours?'

'Very much. It's always good to break old routines. If we had viewer support I'd decided to ask to be moved to those time slots permanently.'

'That sounds as if something has changed your mind, Mr Young.'

He swallowed. 'I have to be very careful to make the right career move. I thought I might be making the decision too quickly.'

David glanced at his watch. 'We'll try to get you away in time for the late news tonight.'

'It's all right, Inspector. The constable upstairs allowed me to phone the studio. I told them there'd been an accident and I was delayed. They'll get a stand-in. Dr Edgely advised me to go home as soon as you'd finished with me.'

'Right.' There was a tap on the door and Reeves broke off. Sergeant Hobbs appeared with a tray laden with milk, sugar, cups and a steaming pot of coffee. He deposited it on the desk and left with a shake of his head at the Inspector's interrogative eyebrow. Andrews came forward and poured a cup for Frank. Reeves poured himself one and motioned me to do the same.

'Were you very close to Madeline Grey?' he continued conversationally.

'No, no, we were colleagues, nothing more.'

'And yet Mr Douglas told us he met you at a party at her house.'

He gave a strained smile. 'Studio politics, Inspector. I was bored stiff and left as soon as I could.'

'So you wouldn't say you knew Mrs Grey well?'

'I saw her quite often in the studios, that's all. I hadn't seen her for a couple of weeks before tonight.'

'Why was that?'

'My time changes. I'm no longer in the studios at the same time as she is. *Kids' World* don't usually tape at weekends unless there's an emergency. I also pre-tape a regular environmental segment called the *Earth Report* but we do a week in one hit and that's arranged to suit my times.'

'So you've had no idea of Mrs Grey's condition over the last couple of weeks.'

'There's always talk, gossip, of course.' He looked troubled. 'And there was that incident on Wednesday. Mr Douglas, Micky, would have told you.'

'I'd like to hear your version, Mr Young.'

Cunning! I told him silently. You know I didn't tell you about that, David.

Frank spoke hesitatingly. 'I was in the make-up room getting ready to tape the *Earth Report*. Micky was being made up for *Kids' World*. There—there'd been rumours, there always are around the studios. Everyone is very interested in everyone else's business. The door to the ironing room was open and Gwen Bright was in there sounding very upset. When the girls realized we could hear her, they closed the door. Of course I'd heard Maddy had left Gwen.'

'And Miss Bright was angry about that?'

He stirred uncomfortably. 'Who wouldn't be? I'm sure it was nothing, really. Mrs Grey, Maddy, was very insecure and unhappy. I'm sure she'd have been sorry later.'

'So Miss Bright wouldn't have been really worried?'

'She knew Maddy. Gwen was just letting off steam. She didn't mean it.'

'What exactly did you overhear, Mr Young?'

'Look, I really don't remember very exactly. Something about Maddy getting what she deserved.' He looked acutely uncomfortable. 'It was just talk.'

'Of course.' David moved him smoothly along.

Frank had arrived at the channel after lunch as usual to be met with the news that Maddy had finally gone mad.

He gave the impression that the details had been forced on him. 'I really don't think it helps to gossip about it.' He'd waited until just after five, then driven down the mountain to Riley's. After buying his book he'd gone down to the garden, deciding to watch the proceedings from the back.

'Why was that?'

'I thought there might be trouble. To tell you the truth, I felt sorry for Maddy and thought I might be of use to her. I wasn't happy to hear all the abuse she was receiving— people putting her down behind her back. I've often felt she was unfairly judged.'

'Did you go to her at all?'

'No, I knew Tony was looking after her and felt, in the circumstances, it was best not to interfere. A woman latched on to me—Miss Fry. She seemed upset about something and kept talking. I couldn't get away from her. Then she said she had something to do and left me. She went up the stairs. I—I needed a drink. The boy poured me a wine and I moved down the garden in case Miss Fry came back and then John Riley started to talk and I sat on the steps about half way down. I didn't feel comfortable. I couldn't concentrate much. In the end, I edged my way back up the garden. It was a mistake. As soon as I'd got back to the stairs the woman grabbed me again. She looked dreadful. I think she'd been crying. She chattered on quite randomly. I was trying to listen to Micky so I only answered her out of courtesy when I felt it would be rude not to.'

'Who was around the stairs at that time?'

He thought back. 'Tony came out of the shadows on my left. There's a stand of tree ferns there casting a very deep shadow. I wondered what he'd been doing. He went over to the drinks table and spent a while getting himself a drink. He came back and stood just in front of me. He was shaking his hand. His sleeve was wet.'

'He didn't go back into the shadows?'

'No, Inspector. He stood in front of me. The boy in

charge of the drinks came down the stairs with a tray of food and went to the table. He started to pour out wine into cups, then came past me again with the ice bucket and went upstairs. A few minutes later he came back down and went to the table again. He seemed to be looking for something. The girl, his sister, apparently, came down the stairs and helped him. They were both looking around—searching under the table. I had the impression they'd lost something. Then she ran very quickly up the stairs and came back with a small hammer. He started to break up the ice. Then Micky finished and Angela ran up the stairs and back down. Jessica Savage was standing behind me on the steps most of the time, I think, although it was just an impression. I didn't turn around and look. Gwen Bright had been standing near Tony Ridgeway. She'd been looking at him a bit strangely, anxious, probably. I expect I'd have looked odd myself. She went back down the garden and I was rescued from Miss Fry's attentions by a couple of women I knew who introduced me to a group of their friends. We got drinks and moved away from the table further to the other side, away from Tony. He got a drink and took it to Becky and they were quickly surrounded by her fans. I farewelled my ladies and joined the others. Most of the people had left and Tony told me what had happened. Micky came up with Gwen and we chatted until Bobby West and Angela came over. Angela asked after Maddy and Tony said she was still asleep. Tony was going to wake her but I said I would.'

'Why did you feel you should wake Mrs Grey?'

'I was fed up,' he said abruptly. 'They'd been talking about Maddy. Tony had just told us how he'd given her a drink to shut her up. He sounded brutal. I thought he might be rough with her.'

'Why didn't Miss Grey wake her mother?'

'Tony had his arm around her, holding her. I think he

might have preferred her not to be—subjected to Maddy if she lost her temper.'

'Can you describe what happened then?'

'I went over to Maddy. She seemed awfully quiet.' Frank leaned forward and put his cup carefully on the desk. His hands were shaking but he kept his deep voice steady. 'I touched her and was shocked to find her so cool. It was quite a warm night. I was going to take off my jacket and put it around her. Then it struck me that something was wrong. She sort of slumped sideways and her head lolled forward. I listened for her breathing and put my hand over her heart. I couldn't feel anything. I tried her pulse, but I knew. I thought she must have had a heart attack. I was furious. They'd been talking about her so casually, saying she brought it on herself and all the time she'd been dead —or dying.' He had sounded remote and mechanical as he described finding Maddy's body. Now his voice rose indignantly.

Frank Young had nothing further to add. He submitted to the search with a wry smile and said he knew the Inspector had his job to do. When he returned, David dismissed him and he left thankfully, his face ashen with the strain.

CHAPTER 17

As the door closed behind Frank David remarked, 'My wife's one of his fans. Says he's got a lovely voice. All these announcer types sound the same to me—even Ridgeway.'

'He was in radio,' I put in, 'years ago.'

'Ah!' David turned to me. 'What was all that about over-hearing Miss Bright at the studio?'

It was my turn to wriggle uncomfortably but I repeated, as best I could, Gwen's angry outburst.

'I find it interesting that Mrs Grey dumped her and yet

Miss Bright seems to have been supporting her strongly this evening.'

'As Becky said, Gwen was following a fairly normal pattern. She'd even started blaming herself for Maddy's hostility.'

'Any idea why Mrs Grey left her?'

'Yes.' I repeated my conversation with Maddy when I'd tried to speak for Gillian.

'So she felt Miss Bright was interfering in her daughter's life by encouraging her to realize her ambitions. I see.' He changed the subject abruptly. 'Would you agree Miss Riley had been visibly upset when she left the office earlier?'

I nodded unhappily. 'Yes, Becky's right. She was crying.'

David nodded. 'Now, perhaps you'd like to tell me what the trouble was between Miss Fry and Mrs Grey that you felt so strongly to involve yourself in?'

I told him. He'd have heard it from someone eventually and at least I gave him an honest account, sticking to the facts. He listened without changing expression, making notes on his pad.

When I'd finished he just said, 'Thank you. That's very clear,' and turned to the Sergeant.

'I rather fancy seeing Mr West. He's got one or two things to explain.'

'Right, sir.'

Bobby made no attempt to hide his anxiety and faced the Inspector with a worried frown.

'I've been thinking and thinking,' he admitted frankly. 'I knew you'd want to know all our movements. What an awful thing to have happened.'

'Were you surprised, Mr West?'

He jumped. 'What do you mean? Of course I was surprised. We all were.'

'Surely, after all the quarrels and bad feelings between Mrs Grey and so many people . . .'

'But you don't expect people to murder people, do you?

Anyway, I know Maddy was being difficult but she was pretty upset. It was my fault.'

'How was it your fault, Mr West?'

He hesitated. 'Look, can I be sure this won't go any further?'

David looked at me. 'Perhaps you'd prefer . . .'

'Oh no, Micky knows already. It's like this, Inspector. I'm in love with Angela Grey. I've kept it secret but I've every reason to think she feels the same. I told Micky on Saturday that Maddy caught us together on Friday night.' He saw David's expression and said hastily, 'No, it wasn't like that, Angela had been crying. I don't know if anyone's told you, but Maddy had her hooks into Gillian Fry and Angela blamed herself. She's really keen on Gillian. I was just comforting her and Maddy came in. She was very cool but she must have been more bothered than I realized.'

'Why did you tell Mr Douglas about this?'

'I was worried. It wasn't like Maddy to be so calm. I told Micky how it was to warn him to keep an eye out for trouble. He's an old family friend of the Greys.'

'What did you expect Mrs Grey to do?'

He bit his lip. 'Well, she could've taken it out on Angie, hit her about. She did, you know, when she was drunk—and she would have tried to separate us. Angie's only fourteen and I wasn't going to say anything to her yet. I'm waiting until she's old enough, so please don't think anything's wrong.'

'I don't, Mr West. Was that the only reason you were worried? Because Miss Grey is under age?'

'No.' Bobby swallowed. 'The truth is, four years ago I—Maddy—' He stopped, embarrassed. 'Look, we had an affair. It's over now. Has been for two years. I can't explain. She—she overwhelmed me and I behaved like a jerk and although I was sick about it for weeks when she called it off, I got over it. The thing is, Maddy didn't always think it was finished. It was she who dropped me, Inspector. I

didn't have the will or the guts, although I knew it wasn't
right. I nearly left the show but Tony talked me into staying. It was the New Year and they were planning the next
series. When I came to my senses I decided I could stay
and just be with Maddy as a fellow actor. Then I found
out she never lets go. She simply didn't accept I wasn't still
in love with her. She'd got another bloke by then but she
wanted me, too—or she wanted me to want her and be
dependent on her. Every now and then she'd remind me,
snuggle up at a party, invite me to dinner and make suggestive remarks in front of everyone. It was pretty awful, but
I thought surely she'd realize I didn't want her any more
and she'd quit. Anyway, I was scared stiff that she'd take
it out on Angie, not because Angela was too young but
because Maddy was jealous of her.'

'Why did you accept Mrs Grey's invitations if it was so
unpleasant?'

'I wanted to see Angela,' Bobby said simply. 'I never let
her know how I felt about her but I took every opportunity
to be with her. At first I thought she just looked on me as
a friend—a sort of older brother—but lately . . .' His eyes
glowed.

'So you believe Mrs Grey became jealous after finding
you with her daughter and fell into an angry rage which
she then proceeded to take out on everybody around her?'

'Well, I can't think of anything else that might have set
her off. I've been really worried about it.'

'I see. Mr West, you were seen going over to Mrs Grey
tonight when she was in the garden. Would you like to tell
me about that?'

'Oh, of course. I went over to see if she was all right. She
—she was asleep. I came away again. I didn't like to wake
her up.'

'How did you know she was in the garden, Mr West?'

'Uh? Miss Savage told me.'

'Would you be a little more explicit?'

'I'm sorry. I went to check up on Maddy. I was about to go up to the office when Miss Savage stopped me. She laughed and said if I was one of the pilgrimage to Maddy I'd save myself a walk if I looked for her in the garden. Then she pointed to a dark corner under some tree ferns. I went over and found her like I said.'

'Asleep and snoring loudly?'

'No.' He looked startled. 'She wasn't snoring. She was just quietly asleep, a little slumped in the chair.'

'You're sure she was asleep, Mr West?'

'Of course. She made little movements in her sleep. And muttered something. She must have been dreaming.'

'Did you go near her again?'

'No.'

'Did you see anyone else around that area?'

'Let me think.' He watched the Inspector for a moment, then he said, 'Of course, I was with Angela all during the launch. We were sitting half way down. I didn't see anything on the back terrace until later. Then, when the speeches were over, Angela said she was going to see her mother and I was stopped by a fan and asked for my autograph. I thought I'd just check everything was all right and, as I said, I went to Maddy myself. Angela obviously hadn't disturbed her and neither did I.'

'What did you do then?'

'I went to find Angela. I saw her with Tony Ridgeway but I got rather swamped by people again. She found me in the end and waited while I signed autographs. She was with me for the rest of the evening.'

David said casually, 'It was Miss Grey who mentioned her mother was snoring as she slept. Are you sure you didn't hear anything.'

'Oh.' Bobby looked taken aback. 'Look, I don't think . . . but, you know, there was a sound like snoring when I was making my way over to the corner. She must have stopped as her head came forward. That would be it. Yes, Angie's right.'

David leaned forward, watching Bobby closely. 'The fact is, Miss Grey didn't disturb her mother because she didn't go to see her until after you had left Mrs Grey.'

Bobby blinked. 'What? That's not true.'

'I'm afraid it is, Mr West. Miss Grey made the same mistake as you did. She went upstairs to the office first, expecting to find her mother there. When she found the office empty she asked Mr Ridgeway where Mrs Grey was. That was when you saw her. She watched you go to Mrs Grey, waited until you had returned, then went to see her mother. She found her asleep and—snoring loudly, according to her statement.

'Oh!' Bobby's eyes were blank for a moment, then he recovered and smiled suddenly. 'That's all right, then. I mean,' he hurried on, 'I thought you'd got it confused. There were so many people coming and going.'

'Did you see anyone else go to Mrs Grey?'

He shook his head. 'I'm afraid not, Inspector. I didn't get away until nearly everyone had left. Then Angela and I joined the others—Micky and the Ridgeways, Gwen Bright, oh, and Frank Davis. It was just after that when Frank discovered Maddy was—had been killed. I can't tell you any more.'

'As you say, it was confusing,' David agreed blandly. 'Are you sure you've told us everything? There's nothing you'd like to add?'

'No, I can't think of anything.'

Bobby willingly submitted to being searched and left, looking almost cheerful. David and Harry exchanged a look.

'Interesting,' David remarked.

'And very relieved, sir. Hasn't realized the implications yet.'

'What?' I was puzzled. 'You don't think Bobby West had

anything to do with it? According to Angela, Maddy was
alive after Bobby left her.'

'That's true,' David said gravely. 'A very devoted pair.'

'They'll be all right now.' I spoke the thought aloud then
wished I hadn't.

'You mean now Mrs Grey can't put a stop to their relationship?'

'David, I don't agree with Bobby,' I said slowly. 'I've
been thinking. Like Tony, I knew Maddy well. I was a
good friend of her husband and I've known Maddy from
the start.'

'What don't you agree with?'

'Well . . .' I thought back. 'Maddy caught them together
but I think she'd known that Angela was attracted to him.
Couldn't have missed it. Maddy watched Angela like a
hawk. It was obvious to me when Angela was in the studio
while Bobby was taping the show. There was a definite
energy between them. Maddy told Tony she didn't like
Angie hanging around the studios. I reckon she thought it
wasn't that serious, but when she saw them on Friday night
she decided it might get out of hand so she took steps to
nip it in the bud. Bobby told me he thought Maddy would
be angry but she wasn't. She got Angela off to bed, told
Bobby to join the other guests and was very sweet to him
later. In fact, she didn't feel threatened. She was jealous of
Angela for her youth and her looks, but it wouldn't have
occurred to her that the child could steal a man from her.
She obviously believed Bobby could still be brought back to
heel whenever she wanted. No, she was more likely amused
rather than angry, but took the warning. She made plans
to remove Angela to a boarding school and get Bobby away.
Whether he would have gone hardly mattered, I should
think. If he'd stayed, Angela would be gone and the field
would be clear for Maddy. With the threat removed, she'd
have no doubt of her own powers. If he did go south for a
while she'd figure he'd owe her and realize how grateful he

was to her for giving him the chance. Either way she couldn't lose. It sounds as if she was in control, handling the situation and getting Tony on side, or so she thought. She'd have been pretty happy.'

'Then what tipped her over the edge?'

'Search me!'

He said, 'No. I think we'll search Miss Bright next,' then smiled at my obvious disapproval of his humour.

CHAPTER 18

I glanced at my watch and was surprised to find it was nearly ten o'clock. I wondered if I was staying out of curiosity or concern for my friends caught up in the horror they were reliving one by one for the Inspector. Once or twice David had glanced at me but I made no move and he didn't suggest I leave. Perhaps it was a help to him to have me there, I thought, but I knew in my heart I wanted to hear everything I could. David's told me before I'm too curious for my own good.

Gwen Bright collapsed into a flood of tears as soon as she entered the office and I pulled the box of tissues across to her.

'Poor Maddy, poor dear Maddy,' she wept. 'If only I'd been kinder to her, given her more support.'

'Are you blaming yourself for her death, Miss Bright?'

The tears stopped abruptly. 'Oh no, I couldn't. I loved Maddy. How dare you even suggest such a thing. To take a knife and—oh!'

David's voice took on a stern note and Gwen seemed instinctively to respond, sitting up and answering him with more composure.

'I want you to tell me exactly what happened when Mrs

Grey was brought into the office at the beginning of this evening.'

'Of course, Inspector. Maddy knew she was behaving very badly and made an effort to pull herself together. Barbara Riley gave her coffee and she drank it and Tony kept talking to her, bracing her up.'

'Did anyone give her anything else at all? Pills? Alcohol?'

'No, no, of course not. What a thing to suggest,' she said indignantly. 'As if we would! When it was obvious she was going to be all right, Barbara and John went out to tell Micky. I wanted to stay but Tony told me there'd been enough fuss and I should go and mingle and act as if everything was normal. Maddy was going to fix her make-up and just sit quietly with Tony until six o'clock, and then come down. Poor Tony. He was devastated when she took a turn. She got cold feet and refused to go on. She must have realized she'd caused people to talk. Oh dear!' She hauled up another tissue and assaulted it with tears.

'Miss Bright—' David's voice cut through her lamentations—'you were seen approaching Miss Grey after she was seated in the garden. Would you like to tell me about that?'

Once again the tears stopped abruptly and she looked warily at him. 'If anyone says I had anything to do with her death . . .' she began, but David held up a hand.

'No one's suggesting anything of the kind. Please answer the question.'

'Oh!' she sniffed, 'I've had a terrible shock.' David remained unmoved. 'Oh, all right!' she snapped. 'I saw Tony take Maddy to the far corner of the garden. I thought I might be able to help. I went to see if there was anything I could do for her but she was asleep.' She looked defiantly at David. 'Asleep, Inspector.'

'Did you try to wake her?'

'Of course not. I let the poor soul have her rest. And that's all I can tell you.'

'Miss Bright, please think carefully. Did you approach Mrs Grey again during the evening?'

She looked frightened. 'No, I tell you, no! Why should I? She was asleep.'

'You were very devoted to Mrs Grey. What could be more natural than to pop back later to make sure your friend was all right.'

'Well, I didn't. Why can't you just accept that?'

The rest of her story agreed with the others. She'd moved down the terraces and after the launch stayed chatting until I'd met with her on my way up and we'd joined the group at the top of the garden.

'Tell me what happened when you called on Mrs Grey last night.'

'What? How did you know?'

'Never mind how, Miss Bright.'

'Oh!' Her eyes filled again and she wailed, 'I've been awful, really awful. After Maddy told me she was leaving me Tony suggested—oh dear—he suggested I talk to Angela about becoming her agent and starting her on a career in television. He said he was going to put Angela in *Kids' World*. I told him I didn't think Maddy would agree to sign the contract but he said he'd got Angela's father's permission. He was very secretive. I know Morgan Grey had ambitions for Angela and I assumed he'd left a document giving approval for her to become an actress if she wanted. He adored that child. She was just four years old when Morgan died. He wanted the world for her.'

And knew Maddy wouldn't let her have it, I thought.

'So I offered my services to Angela,' Gwen continued. 'I admit it was done in a fit of pique. Angela was sceptical. She said her mother would never let her. I told her Morgan had made provision for her. She was thrilled. Then I felt terrible, going behind Maddy's back. I knew she didn't mean all the things she said. It was all my fault for betraying her trust and encouraging Angela. I begged her to forgive me, let me work for her again. She asked me to come over and discuss a new contract. But—but—' she clutched the tissue box—'when I arrived she was f-furious with me,' Gwen sobbed. 'She knew I'd seen Angela. The child must have told her. Tony certainly wouldn't have. He knew better than to upset her. He was already behind schedule with Maddy's segments and she'd only just got back to work. He was handling her with kid gloves. I feel awful. Now I'll never be able to make it up to her. When Frank Young said she was dead, I was shattered! He hadn't any reason to be so upset about it,' she added spitefully, 'he's only known her for a couple of years. I've been with her from the start. And he had a colossal row with her, you know.'

David leaned forward. 'You're saying Mr Young had a row with Mrs Grey?'

'Yes, I am.' Gwen drew herself up indignantly. 'He's pretending to be so cut up about Maddy, but Tracey, Maddy's secretary, told me today that Frank went to see Maddy last night and they were really yelling at each other.'

'Did Mrs Grey's secretary overhear the conversation?'

'She certainly did—part of it, anyway. She told me they were fighting about Morgan.'

David looked nonplussed. 'Mrs Grey and Mr Young were fighting about Morgan Grey?' he repeated blankly.

'Yes, so you can see Frank knows a lot more than he lets on. I didn't know he even knew Morgan, but Tracey said Maddy told him that if he didn't do exactly what she wanted she'd tell the world the truth about him and Angela's father. And Frank said it would ruin his marriage and he'd stop her any way he had to. Tracey said it made her blood run cold to hear him.'

'How did Mrs Grey's secretary come to overhear this row? Does she work on a Sunday?'

'No, but she'd left some papers behind on Saturday. She

thought Maddy would be cross if she knew, so she slipped in quietly to pick them up. The living-room door was closed and she could hear voices raised as she was in the office across the hall.'

'She's sure it was Mr Young?'

'It was his voice. And she knew Maddy had an appointment with Frank last night.'

'Did she know why?'

'No—' Gwen sounded regretful—'but it was in Maddy's diary. You'd better ask him. He's certainly hiding something.'

There was very little more to be got out of Gwen. She continually blamed herself for distressing her oldest friend and agreed to be searched with a martyred expression as if atoning for her sins. David sent her home with obvious relief.

My friend sat in silent contemplation of the window until Andrews reappeared grinning like a Cheshire Cat.

'It's the redoubtable Miss Savage,' he said gleefully. 'She's just arrived upstairs. Said she was just passing and thought she'd look in. Brian's asked her to wait.'

'It's at times like this,' David said with feeling, 'that I believe in a Higher Intelligence. Wheel her in, Harry!'

'Er—Miss Fry is cutting up rough. She's complaining about police disregard for the comfort of others. She also claims that we bully street kids.'

'Oh yes, the teenagers' author. Convey my apologies, tell her we're churning through them like a sausage machine and we'll be with her very soon—and get the Riley boy to give 'em coffee.'

'Sausage machine?' Harry queried.

'Forget the sausages. Good God, Sergeant, you do it easily enough with her teenage readers. Work your magic on their champion.'

'The coffee'll probably do it.' Harry winked at Constable Shaw who was hiding a smile and departed at top speed.

Jessica Savage strode into the office, her vivid copper hair matching the Inspector's red thatch.

'What brings you back, Miss Savage?'

She looked at him coolly and took a gold cigarette case from her small beaded clutch purse.

'Do you mind?' she asked sweetly and lit a cigarette with a matching gold lighter. She deliberately returned the case and lighter to her bag before answering.

'I'm waiting,' David reminded her. 'We don't have all night to waste, Miss Savage.'

'Of course you don't, Inspector.' She blew the smoke away from her eyes and settled back. 'But you'll be glad my curiosity got the better of me. Your lovely Sergeant Hobbs told me the news. At the risk of sounding like a cliché, you really could have knocked me down with a feather. My God, who am I going to swipe at in my column now? Maddy was so reliable. She was always good for a dig.'

'Miss Savage, I believe I asked you why you returned.'

'Don't get cross, Inspector,' she drawled maddeningly. 'Just thank your lucky stars I did. Actually, after the launch, and having no idea of the dramatic goings-on—I must be losing my journo's instinct for a story—yes, Inspector, I'm telling you—after the launch I went to have dinner with friends of mine. We went to Henri's, down the road. I live at Bardon so I was on my way home and saw lights blazing where all should be dark, police cars parked all over the place and Micky's distinctively decrepit Ford Capri still outside the shop. My nose insisted I investigate, and you're not at all pleased with me—but you should be. I can give you two perfect suspects for your murder.'

CHAPTER 19

Satisfied that she had David's full attention, Jessica told her story with alacrity. She'd arrived at the shop at twenty past five and had spent some minutes browsing through the latest releases and watching the guests come in, spotting anyone who might be good for an interview. She'd seen Maddy's party arrive and realized by their expressions something was wrong. She'd managed to get close enough to overhear their conversation with Fiona who was at the counter and she'd waited with delight for the next scene in the drama. Tony and John had brought Maddy in and Jessica had watched them take her down the stairs and then had tried to pump Fiona to no avail. She'd heard John say they were taking Maddy to the office and she knew where it was.

'I'm often here for book launches to interview the celebrities. And I must say, Riley's rates as my favourite bookshop. Especially after tonight!'

'So you know the layout well, Miss Savage?'

'It's my second home, Inspector.' She gave him an innocent look and continued.

'Obviously I wasn't going to move from the stairs. It's a wonderful vantage-point. I went once down to the garden. Don gave me a drink and I flew right back to my perch. It was quite a party. The Fry woman jumped out of her skin every time she saw me. She doesn't like me, Inspector and I can't think why because I'm really very charming when you get to know me. That lovely Frank Young was waiting around as well, with the same obvious purpose but not, as we all know, for the same reason. The poor pet was pounced on by Fry. Couldn't get away. Frank's such a gentleman, it'll be his undoing. He didn't tell her to rack off, although

it was quite clear he'd have liked to. Answered her in mono-
syllables but she didn't take the hint. Suddenly Fry let
him go and came haring back up the stairs, hovered like a
demented crane-fly on the verandah and then retreated up
to the shop, nervy as hell. Frank got himself a drink and
bolted, as you would, honour finally overcome by the fear
of another Fry attack and the next minute out they all came
—John and Barbara, looking distinctly relieved and Gwen,
probably kicked out by Tony because she was very reluctant and started hovering herself. I hope to God it's not
catching. Finally she made up her mind and came down
the steps. Such a look she gave me. Daggers, Inspector,
daggers. You'll be delighted to know I stood my ground
undaunted.'

'Why will I be delighted, Miss Savage?'

'Dear man, wait just a moment, I'm nearly there. Now,
everyone was off the verandah by then. I could hear
Maddy's voice, very agitated and shrill and Tony's, just a
murmur. Hello! I thought. La Grey is cutting up rough
again. Then Tony came out looking like murder—oops,
sorry! I definitely did not mean to put any ideas in your
head. Everyone at some time or other has worn the same
look around Maddy, I promise you. Especially myself, with
good reason. You must be aware of the next set of events.
Now, here's something you don't know. Rebecca had just
begun her speech when Fry comes back down from the
shop. She looks at Rebecca, her mouth hanging open, looks
at the office door, gives a sort of gasp, then in she goes.
Like Flynn, Inspector, right into the office.'

She sat back, a triumphant look on her face.

Reeves's voice was calm. 'What did you do then, Miss
Savage?'

'Well! Aren't you even a little stirred? I did what any
good journalist would do. I went to the loo.'

'I'm sure you'll explain why.'

'I thought the reason would jump out and bite you. I

went to the loo because it's next to the office and you can overhear everything. Found that out years ago. Fry and La Grey were having the most tremendous row. Well, Fry was. Maddy sounded half cut—very muzzy, I'd say, but the Fry was getting stuck in. Called her a wicked woman, said she'd never give in to her, that she, Fry, would make her, Grey, sorry until her dying day—which, with hindsight, wasn't a long time. Possibly Fry knew that. She sounded very ugly. Then she cried out "What is the matter with you?" in a frustrated way and ran out. I nipped out of the loo by the side door in time to see her make it to the garden. Don poured her a glass of Château Cardboard and she drank it straight down and got another. What do you think of that, Inspector?'

'That's very interesting, Miss Savage. What was the other thing you wanted to tell me?'

She stubbed out her cigarette impatiently. 'My God, not even a flicker of excitement, and you with hair as fiery as mine! I sense we're not destined to be soul mates and you're going to be boringly prosaic. All right, have it your way. After Fry flew away Miss Riley came down from the shop. She went into the office. Words were spoken. Angry words. Before I had time to go to the Ladies again it was all over. Fiona rushed out in floods of tears, slammed the door and ran back up to the shop. It really was the most marvellous evening. I must come to your launches more often, Michael. I had no idea they could be so productive. Within minutes Maddy, now presumably thoroughly wound up after two cat fights, came staggering down the stairs. She smelt strongly of alcohol. I watched with bated breath but, sadly, Tony deflected her and took her away. He got her a drink from what I could see, although I think she'd had quite enough. Poor dear Tony. Maddy was muttering to herself and started into him.'

'Did you overhear what she was saying?'

'Sadly, not a lot, and it wasn't for the sake of trying as

I'm sure you'd be aware. She sounded abusive and said something about Angela's precious father. Of course I pricked up my ears because Morgan Grey was once very precious to me. She said she'd expose something or other but of course Michael was chatting on and he's a funny man, Inspector, so there was a lot of laughing which quite ruined my chances of hearing any more. I gather Maddy wanted to go down and launch the book, not grasping the fact that it had already been impressively launched by Rebecca. I've got a lot of time for Rebecca Ridgeway. She deserves all the good life can give her and she doesn't even know it. Anyway, before you bring me sternly back to the point, Tony told her, all right, she could go down and get it off her chest but she should sit and have a drink first.'

The rest of Jessica's story held nothing we didn't know. Tony had gone for a drink and had taken it back to the stairs. Frank Young was behind him talking to Gillian. 'Would you believe, poor Frank came back to his post and got Fryed again!' Don had come down from the kitchen with a tray of food, Gwen Bright had gone to Maddy and returned, 'She hung around Tony for a bit then pushed off,' Don had run back up the stairs with the empty ice bucket, returning in minutes with more ice. Fiona had come down, 'looking seriously worried, Inspector,' and had then run back up to the kitchen for a small hammer. I'd finished answering questions, Angela had been next to run up to the office and back down immmediately. Bobby began to come up the stairs to be told by Jessica that Maddy was now in the garden.

'He dithered a bit, fortified himself with a drink, then marched resolutely into the shadows. He came out minutes later and young Angela dived in to see her mother, although why she'd want to, I can't imagine.'

'Where was Miss Fry during all this?'

'She had Frank torn from her by some other women. Fair's fair, Inspector. After all, when a man is so exceedingly attractive, it's only right to share him around, don't you think so, Sergeant?' She gave Harry a limpid look but he preserved a wooden front. 'I didn't notice her after that. If she hadn't been behaving so oddly I'd have barely noticed her at all. She has a way of merging into the background. Useful. I should cultivate it. She could have gone and taken a knife to Maddy and I'll bet no one would have seen her.'

'What about Don Riley? I gather he was missing for quite a time from the drinks table.'

'He was working. Taking trays of nibbles around—the top terrace, anyway. Michael drew such a crowd you couldn't get down further. He was in the kitchen during all the drama. Cutting up more ham and cheese and salady things, I suppose. He can wield a knife like an expert. He'd gone up with a couple of empty plates just before Miss Riley did her bit towards the evening's entertainment.'

'Did you notice him going over to Mrs Grey?'

'No, but I wasn't watching him particularly. He might have, but would he know she was there?'

'Perhaps he heard her snoring or muttering in her sleep.'

'Well, if he did, he's got good ears. There wasn't a sound from her corner. I'd have said she was out like a light.'

'Miss Savage, I want you to be very sure about this. Was Mrs Grey drunk when she came past you on her way down to the garden?'

'She was extremely tired and emotional, Inspector. As a newt!' She smiled suddenly at David. 'I gather you don't find my suspects convincing enough. Well, I'll give you this for free. While Don Riley was smashing up ice his charming sister was taking a tray of goodies around. She was right next to me when I told Pretty Boy West where to find his quarry. I helped myself to some eats and the girl looked, well, "murderous" springs to mind. She kept her eyes on the fatal corner, let me tell you, and about five minutes after Angela Grey came out, Miss Riley went back to the table, deposited her tray and very purposely followed the now well worn trail into the bushes. So now you know!'

David seemed to hold her eyes with his. She met his look squarely. After a moment he spoke abruptly.

'Did you at any time leave the steps and go over to Mrs Grey yourself?

'I did not.'

'You had every reason to want her dead, I've been told.'

'Then you've been told wrong, Inspector. I had no reason at all. I hated Maddy's guts. She took a beautiful man and wrecked his life. I can completely understand why anyone would succumb to the urge to murder her and later I'll drink a toast to them and wish them all the very best. But I'd have preferred her live and squirming for a good many more years. It was a much more fitting punishment and I enjoyed it. I didn't kill her. I'm sorry she's dead. Believe it or not as you please.'

'Vindictive bitch!' Harry said as the door closed behind Jessica.

'Prolonged hatred is a very dangerous habit,' David said, echoing Becky. 'I must say I found Miss Savage entertaining. I read her column myself. She can dig that pen of hers in very deep. I don't think she did it, though. I believe her when she says she'd have preferred Mrs Grey alive. And she's too striking. Someone would have noticed her crossing the terrace. We'll take Miss Fry now, Harry, before she files a formal complaint.'

CHAPTER 20

I don't especially like Jessica Savage but I had to admit her description of Gillian Fry was accurate. She really did give the impression of a crane-fly, long legs stuck awkwardly at angles as she sat, hands waving uncertainly.

'It's about time, Inspector. Keeping us all upstairs for-ever!' she began. David cut through her protest.

'Miss Fry, you are far more comfortable here than you would be at the police station. We are working as swiftly as possible and we have heard some very serious allegations against you. I suggest you answer my questions as accu-rately as possible and don't waste our time.'

Gillian's mouth closed with shock. She looked at me uncertainly. 'Micky?'

'It's all right, Gillian,' I said and thought: Bloody hell, why do I keep saying that? It's not all right and it looks bad for Gilly. 'Just answer the Inspector and you'll be OK.'

She faced David. 'I'm sure I don't know what you mean, but I've got nothing to hide.'

'Miss Fry, you're known to have been involved in a seri-ous dispute with the deceased. You made it clear you intended to continue to fight her. She was ready to ruin you. Mr Young has told us you were upset and left him saying you "had something to do". Miss Savage states you were nervy and that you went into the office and accosted Mrs Grey. You were heard to call her a "wicked woman" and tell her that you would "make her sorry until her dying day". You left in a very agitated state. Later you had been crying and, according to Mr Young, "looked dreadful". No one has remembered seeing you between six-forty-five and seven p.m., which would have given you ample time to carry out your threat. You were presumably around the top terrace when Mrs Grey came down and I'm sure you saw where she was sitting. Do you have anything to say?'

I felt sorry for Gillian. She drooped like a deflated clown, a hand over her eyes as if to blot out David's face. He waited.

'Well, Miss Fry?'

She raised her head and her voice rose hysterically. 'I didn't kill her. I didn't, I didn't!' David jerked his head towards the kitchen and Harry brought her a drink of water which she gulped down. 'It's true I told her off,' she said more quietly. 'She was a wicked woman. She was quite deliberately setting out to stop my book, destroy my reputation. But I didn't kill her, I swear it.'

'Tell me why you quarrelled with her this evening.'

'I was worried,' she said in a low voice. 'I thought perhaps I could talk to her, change her mind. I was scared but I was determined to see it through. I went into the office. She was sitting with her back to me. I spoke to her but she didn't even do me the courtesy of turning around. I introduced myself. I'd made up my mind I'd be calm but she started talking, muttering threats. She'd expose me, she said. I couldn't go behind her back and get away with it. She sounded strange, half mad. I was terrified. I—I shook her. She was so limp and odd. Then she seemed to see me. It was as if she was in some distant dream state. She turned and focused on me and said, "Who the hell are you?" I was in a blaze by then. She was doing it deliberately, to rile me. Well, she succeeded. But she wasn't rational at all. Said she'd send her daughter away rather than let me influence her. I couldn't get any sense out of her. She was crazy. I —I lost my nerve and ran out. I was terribly upset. I seemed to have brought more trouble on that sweet child. I suddenly realized I couldn't argue with a crazy woman. She reeked of drink. I went back into the garden. I was shaking. I normally don't drink much alcohol but I got a glass of wine and drank it, then took another. I couldn't stop my hands trembling. Then I saw the nice man I'd been talking to earlier and I joined him.'

'What did you do when his attention was taken by the other women?'

She gave him a miserable look. 'I felt rather sick and I went across to a bench beyond the drinks table. There was a space and I sat down next to a nice woman with a floral dress and a lovely shawl. She told me she'd embroidered it herself. I don't know her name—Julie, I think, or Judy.

She'd remember me. I honestly didn't see Maddy Grey
come down. When people started to move I saw Angela
Grey in the garden. I wanted to tell her what I'd done, that
I'd caused her more grief, but someone recognized me and
asked me to sign one of my books. Then I was talking to
some young people for a while. I waited to say good night
to Micky, and then Angela came up and I tried to speak to
her but there were too many people around. Then Mr
Young went to wake Maddy. Oh!' She gave a heartfelt cry
and covered her face with both hands.

David questioned her some more but she'd been too
wrapped up in her troubles to notice anyone else's movements. Finally he let her go after dealing briskly with her
half-hearted accusations of police brutality on being asked
to go with Constable Shaw to be searched.

'Well!' David leaned back and swung his chair gently back
and forth, deep in thought. 'What do you reckon, Harry?'

'Where did Mrs Grey get the drink?'

'Exactly. It's been obvious from the start—from your
statement, Micky, that Mrs Grey was drunk when she came
out of the office and yet, half an hour before, she'd been,
according to four witnesses, sober enough to launch the
book and apologize for her behaviour. No one admits to
giving her anything and indeed, as Miss Bright said, who'd
do a thing like that? It was to everyone's advantage to have
Mrs Grey on deck, performing for Channel 6.' He paused
and looked at his watch. 'We've got a long night ahead of
us. How's Brian going?'

'He thinks he's got it.' Harry joined his boss and they
turned away from me. I couldn't make out the object, neatly
bagged in plastic, that the Sergeant pulled out of his jacket
pocket.

'Any prints? Blood?'

'As you see, sir, it's as clean as a whistle now. Don Riley
washed it up with the other things. Brian's got a collection
of knives and a couple of screwdrivers from a tool-box,

but they're clean, too. He rang George Thengalis. George reckons this'd fit the wound to a T. Brian says do you want him to do the other room?'

Reeves had transferred whatever it was to a drawer in the desk and shook his head.

'This is it, Harry, I'll bet you anything you like. We'll get it to George, ASAP.'

'Another thing,' Harry told him, 'George confirmed the stabbing caused the death but there was also bruising to the deceased's throat and jaw. Almost as if someone had tried to strangle her first.'

David's mobile eyebrows went up. 'Oh? In order to make her lose consciousness before the actual stabbing?'

'Why, if she was already out to it?'

'Good point. And the alcohol?'

'Unclear, given that she'd imbibed a large amount during the day. But he said he did feel the amount still in the stomach was disproportionate to the time which had presumably elapsed between the last drink at home before the Ridgeways picked her up and the one glass of wine Mr Ridgeway admits to having given her.'

'Meaning?' Reeves said impatiently.

'Meaning, sir, that when Brian pinned him down he said he wouldn't like to swear that she hadn't had a good swig of Scotch not long before she was killed, but he wasn't in any sort of position to confirm that and why the hell didn't we leave him to get on with his job.'

David grinned. 'Ah!'

'Exactly, sir. I'd say you were right about the drink.'

'Well, let's find out, Harry. I'll have the Rileys in together. They'd be likely to shield each other singly. All together, they'll give themselves away. Have Brian join us and we'll see what we'll see.'

Brian and Harry set extra chairs and the Rileys sat around the desk. I moved back to give them room.

'I'm sorry to have left you until last,' David said and smiled at them. 'I expect you'll be glad to see the back of us.'

'What's happening, Inspector?' John asked tiredly. 'Have you found out who did it?'

'These things take time, Mr Riley. We've over a hundred people to interview to confirm statements and gather all the evidence. I thought it would save a lot of time if I saw you all together and then you can get off home. Does anyone object?'

They looked at each other. Barbara leaned towards John and squeezed his hand.

'No one has anything private to tell me that you'd prefer not to say in front of the others?'

'We were all working,' Barbara said. 'How could we be involved?'

'Right, then we'll get on. Mrs Riley, I gather you weren't in the garden during the launch.'

She smoothed her skirt composedly. 'No, Inspector, I was working in the shop. When we have a book launch or an evening function, we don't close the door. We stay open for latecomers and people coming to pick people up afterwards and we serve any customers who come in.'

'But you were on the verandah earlier.'

'Yes. Fiona was upstairs early in the evening and I was outside with a table of Micky's books and a money box and credit card machine. When I was asked to look after Mrs Grey I called Fiona down and she took over from me. We left the shop to take care of itself for a while—' she smiled —'not being able to be in two places at once. There were still plenty of people upstairs arriving for the launch, so I didn't think anyone would rob the till. The minute I could leave Mrs Grey, when she'd recovered sufficiently, I went back upstairs and stayed there.'

'Serving customers?'

'What a lovely thought. No, only one or two people came

in. I was working—tidying, topping up books, making up mail orders. The work never stops, Inspector.'

'And you didn't come down again at any time?'

'No, not until I was told of Mrs Grey's death. Then I joined the others in the office. We closed the shop, of course, and later your constable was stationed at the door.'

David turned to John. 'Mr Riley, would you agree Mrs Grey was in a capable condition when you left her in the office? Capable of doing her job?'

'Definitely.' He nodded briskly. 'Babs gave her coffee and she seemed all right.'

'Did anyone give her anything else at all?'

He looked surprised. 'Like what? You mean something in the coffee? I didn't see anyone do that.'

'I mean alcohol, Mr Riley.'

His reaction was identical to Tony's. He stared at David in disbelief.

'Who'd do a crazy thing like that? Absolutely not, Inspector.'

'Then can you explain—any of you—how Mrs Grey consumed a large amount of alcohol, possibly whisky, which made her so drunk that she could hardly walk down the stairs just thirty minutes later?'

They looked at each other, startled. Barbara said faintly, 'Oh my God, the cabinet!' John stood abruptly and crossed the room, closely followed by Sergeant Hobbs. He opened a small cabinet behind his desk. Hobbs said, 'Excuse me, sir, I'll take that,' and took out a handkerchief, with which he gently protected the half-empty bottle of Johnnie Walker he held up.

'We don't serve it at functions,' John said. 'I keep it for special occasions—if I'm entertaining authors or publishers, one or two friends in the media. We got new supplies in yesterday. This bottle was full.'

CHAPTER 21

Barbara looked shocked. 'You mean Maddy Grey went straight to the cabinet as soon as she was left alone and—oh no!'

John shook his head as Brian carefully placed the bottle on the desk. 'We might have guessed, you know. Tony Ridgeway said her nerve snapped. What would be more likely than her taking her usual way out?'

'Could she have known where you kept the whisky?' Reeves cut in.

'She must have searched the office,' Barbara said. 'Alcoholics are supposed to have an instinct for finding the stuff.'

'That explains her condition when Miss Fry accosted her,' David remarked. 'She said Mrs Grey ignored her, was muttering threats, half mad. She'd thought it was a deliberate attempt on Mrs Grey's part to anger her. Is that the way she seemed to you, Miss Riley?'

Fiona jumped. 'I don't know what you mean.'

'Surely you do. When you confronted Mrs Grey here in the office just before six-thirty.'

Barbara went over to Fiona and put an arm around her. 'What are you saying, Inspector? Fiona was in the shop with me. She came up as soon as the launch started.'

'It's all right, Mum.' Fiona sat straight in her chair and faced Reeves. 'I didn't know anyone saw me.'

'Tell me about it, Miss Riley.'

She hesitated, looking around the rest of her family before she turned back to David.

'I was angry because she'd refused to let us have the *Kids' World* franchise. We really need it or we'll be in financial trouble. I thought about it for a while. I thought perhaps I could talk to her. I knew she was in the office. I was

still on the verandah when Mr Ridgeway came out alone
and Rebecca Rowland took over the launch. I decided to
go down and see if I could at least make her understand
what she was doing to us. So I waited until Mum was in
the back room in the shop and I slipped downstairs.' She
leaned against her mother's arm. 'I'm sorry, Mum. It was
a stupid idea. I went in and Mrs Grey was obviously drunk
and very angry about something. She didn't seem to know
where she was or what was happening but when she saw
me she sort of came to and recognized me. She said I was
one of that family of—of vipers—and she'd make us sorry
for ever supporting Gillian Fry. I said she couldn't do any
worse than she'd done and—and—'

'Yes, Miss Riley?' David leaned forward, his voice gentle.
'What did she say to that?'

A tear ran down Fiona's face. She brushed it away and
stared helplessly at him. 'She said she knew who owned the
shop. She'd made it her business to find out. She said he
was thinking of selling and she was going to buy the building and throw us out!' She broke down and sobbed while
Barbara soothed her, a distressed look on her face.

'Oh, there, there, darling. Don't worry. My poor girl.'

Fiona shakily found a handkerchief in her pocket and
wiped her eyes. 'I couldn't say anything,' she whispered.
'She was horrible. She looked so spiteful. Then she started
to get up and come towards me. She was hanging on to the
desk. I was terrified. I ran out of the office and back up to
the shop. Mum saw I was crying but I said I was still upset
about losing the franchise. I didn't want to worry her any
more.'

Barbara rocked her gently. 'Oh, Fi, I wish you'd said.'

David watched her, his expression hard to read. 'Miss
Riley, I'm sorry to have to distress you further but this
makes it very difficult for me. Did you tell any other
member of your family about your conversation with Mrs
Grey?'

'No I didn't.'

'You didn't tell your brother when you were together?'

'No, honestly I didn't.'

'I have to tell you that you were seen going over to Mrs Grey when she was in the garden after you had come down from the shop. This puts you in rather a serious position. Do you have anything to say?'

Fiona was white. 'I didn't kill her.'

'So far I haven't suggested that you did. Did you continue your quarrel with Mrs Grey?'

'No.' Fiona bit her lip and twisted her damp hanky. 'I —I did go over. I wanted to ask her please not to hurt us any more. I felt dreadful. It was my fault she'd decided to buy the shop.'

'Did you speak to her?'

'She was asleep. I stood and looked at her. It was dark but there was enough light from the garden to see. Suddenly I thought she looked really pathetic. I don't expect you'll believe me but I felt sorry for her. Everyone hated her and she was sad and drunk and sour and awful. I thought, what's the use, and I just turned around and left her there.'

'You didn't touch her? Speak to her?'

'No. I only wanted to get away from her. Micky had finished signing books and I got him a drink and something to eat and took it down to him.'

'I see. Thank you, Miss Riley.'

'Do you believe me?'

David looked at her for a moment. 'Possibly. We've a way to go yet.' He turned to John.

'Mr Riley, you were in the gazebo with Mr Douglas and Mrs Ridgeway. Did you notice your daughter coming out of the office?'

John compressed his lips and finally gave a little gesture of surrender.

'Yes, I did. I heard a door slam. I looked up. I could see Fi was crying.'

'Did you ask her why?'

'No, I didn't get the chance but I knew it must have been something that woman had said to her. I felt . . .' He stopped.

'You felt like what?'

'If you must know, I felt like killing her.'

'You must have seen Mrs Grey coming out of the office.'

'No, but Micky told me she was on the loose when he handed over to me. I called for questions and was looking out for people with their hands up, but I didn't see Mrs Grey. After the questions I left the gazebo.'

'You went to the back of the garden?'

'No, I stayed close by, talking to people. I felt edgy. I wanted to wait until Micky had finished, just in case Mrs Grey came down and tried to make trouble.'

'So you didn't go near the back corner?'

'No,' he repeated. 'When Micky had finished signing I tidied up the gazebo, put the microphone away, straightened the chairs and collected the glass and jug. I helped Don go around the lower terraces picking up glasses and checking no one had left things—bags, books—you'd be amazed what people will go home without. I got to the top terrace just as Gillian Fry screamed. Then I went to see what the trouble was.'

'Can anyone support your story?'

'I can,' Don said quickly, 'Dad was in my sight all the time.'

'Apparently you weren't so lucky, Mr Riley. There were several periods when you were away from the drinks table and no one can say where you were.'

Don shrugged. 'I was serving—taking a tray around as far as I could get. I was upstairs for a while cutting up more ham and salami. It was quite a big crowd tonight. I didn't even know Maddy Grey had left the office until Fi told me later.'

David considered him. 'Tell me about your movements

later in the evening. You and Miss Riley were seen searching for something and then she ran up the stairs and
returned with a hammer with which you broke up some
ice. Is that your normal practice?'

'No. We use an ice pick. It's only small but it's sharp.
I'd used it earlier when I set the drinks up before the launch
but it disappeared. The ice bucket was empty and I ran
upstairs and brought more ice down, then I couldn't find
the pick. So Fi got a hammer from the tool kit.'

'Do you use a lot of ice?'

'No, I should have brought down enough but the bucket
had fallen over and it was empty.'

'Did you find the ice pick?'

'Yes, eventually. It had slipped off the table into a box
underneath with the empty wine casks and used glasses. I
didn't find it until I was putting everything away and washing up.'

'And you hadn't missed it earlier?'

'Not until I needed it. I didn't realize it had fallen off the
table.'

'You washed everything up very carefully, even the ice
pick?'

He stared. 'Yes. How did you know?'

David brought the sealed plastic bag out of his pocket.
'Is this the ice pick, Mr Riley?'

They all gasped. Don nodded. 'Yes.'

Barbara gave a faint moan and said, 'Oh no!'

'I'm afraid so, Mrs Riley. Your ice pick appears to be
the murder weapon.'

CHAPTER 22

The Rileys looked at he silver ice pick with distaste. David laid it on the desk.

'We'll take this with us. It will be returned to you in due course.'

Fiona looked faint. 'I don't ever want to see it again,' she said.

'Now, Mr Riley.' David turned back to Don. 'You took everything into the kitchen and washed it before we arrived. Didn't Dr Edgely warn you not to touch anything?'

'I didn't think,' Don said awkwardly. 'I knew *she* shouldn't be touched. I needed something to do—to occupy myself with. It's automatic to just get on and tidy up. I didn't think it would apply to food and cups and plates.'

'And knives?'

'Yes, sorry. It really didn't occur to me that she might have been stabbed by anything of ours. I had a vague idea someone had brought a penknife or something.'

'Did you notice anything at all unusual? Especially on the ice pick? Blood, tissue, stains of any sort?'

Don swallowed. 'No, no, nothing like that,' he said hastily. 'It was just the same as always. It was quite clean. Not—not messy in any way.'

'And the knives?'

'Yes. They were in the kitchen anyway. All the preparation's done upstairs. The knives weren't taken downstairs.'

'And yet anyone passing through the kitchen would have seen them?'

'On the sink, yes.'

'You've made a lot of trouble for us, Mr Riley,' David said sternly. 'We only have your word for it that you didn't know where Mrs Grey was and that you didn't approach her. You've effectively destroyed any evidence of blood and fingerprints on the probable murder weapon, which is suspicious enough in itself. You had ample opportunity to go to the corner of the garden, murder Mrs Grey and return unnoticed. No one was paying you any particular attention as you moved around. What is more, you very clearly knew your sister had seen Mrs Grey and of her threat to close the shop.'

'I didn't!' Don was white around the mouth.

'I think you must have, Mr Riley. We have evidence that you took a couple of empty plates to the kitchen before Miss Riley spoke to Mrs Grey in the office and you didn't return until Mrs Grey had gone down to the garden. There's no way you couldn't have overheard their quarrel.'

'You're right.' Don's voice was husky. 'I did hear Fi and that—Mrs Grey. I didn't say anything to Fi. I wanted to wait and talk it over later when everyone was calmer and the people had gone. There was a big crowd and we'd run low on food. As soon as I could I came up to refill the plates for after the launch. I heard Fi and I opened the door a crack and listened. When I heard Mrs Grey threaten to close us down I was going to come into the office and confront her myself, but Fi ran out and I realized there was no point, in her condition she wouldn't have been rational.'

'What did you do then?'

'I finished preparing the food and took the tray back down to the garden. Honestly.' He looked anxiously at David.

'Right.' David's face relaxed. 'Don't worry, Mr Riley, I'm not about to drag you away in handcuffs. For the moment I accept your story. Did you go anywhere in the direction of the tree ferns in your travels?'

Don looked wary. 'Once or twice.'

'Tell me—and try to get it right, Mr Riley—did you hear anything—any sound at all from that corner?'

'No, nothing.'

'Did you see anyone there?'

'Only a figure sitting in the gloom. I didn't know it was Mrs Grey. I didn't go that close. It could have been anyone just wanting to sit down. I wasn't looking in particular.'

'Do you still say you didn't know Mrs Grey came downstairs?'

'I promise, I really didn't know. When Fi ran out I closed the door and got on with my work. I didn't hear Mrs Grey go out and I didn't see her when I came back down. I thought she was still in the office.'

'All right.' David spent a few moments writing in his notebook, then he looked up gravely.

'We'll probably want to question you all again to corroborate statements and as the picture becomes more clear. If anything occurs to you, if you remember anything at all which may have any bearing on this, no matter how insignificant it may seem to you—someone looking odd, anyone near Mrs Grey, anyone handling the ice pick, please let me know at once. In the meantime you can finish whatever you need to do here and shut up shop for the night. We'll be on our way shortly. Thank you.'

As the Rileys, looking rather dazed, left the office David turned to Sergeant Andrews. 'Send Bates down, Harry.'

Constable Bates arrived with speed, grinned at the Inspector and took out a notebook.

'Let's have it, Col.'

'Yessir! Very little conversation upstairs, they were all very conscious of my presence. Mr Young requested to telephone his studio. He made one call stating he had been delayed due to an accident and would not be available tonight. Miss Grey was very calm before and after her interview. She said nothing except when she came back and sat very close to Mr West. He looked troubled and she said, "Don't worry, Bobby, everything will be all right." Mrs Ridgeway was also very quiet when she returned saying only, "My God, I hope this is over soon." She said this to the room in general. Mr Ridgeway seemed restless. He said he had a lot of work to do and should be phoning people right now. When he returned he said to Miss Bright, "Thanks for keeping shtum about Maddy being downstairs. We've got a lot to discuss. I'll call you tomorrow." Miss Bright answered, "I don't know what to do. You'll have to advise me." Mr Ridgeway replied, "Don't worry, Gwenny, you'll be all right." As the Ridgeways and Miss Grey were leaving Mr West said to Miss Grey, "Don't blame yourself, Angela. It wasn't your fault." Mr Young left without comment as did Mr West. Miss Savage arrived while Miss Bright was with you, sir, and demanded to know what was happening. I called down to Sergeant Hobbs, not knowing what to do. He explained the situation and she said she had important information and was very insistent that she speak to you. When Miss Bright came back she was extremely put out to see Miss Savage. "You're a heartless bitch," she said to her, "and I hope someone makes you sorry for what you've done." Miss Savage just laughed. She spoke to Miss Fry before she left. "You've got your wish, then," she said. Miss Fry replied in a shocked way, "How could you, how do we know you didn't do it yourself?" Miss Savage seemed to find that very funny and I advised her to leave if she had no other business.' He stopped and looked embarrassed.

'Yes, Col?'

'Nothing pertinent to the case, sir.'

'Let's have it, Constable.'

'Well, sir, Miss Savage—er—patted me on the cheek, sir, and said, "Only if you come, too, handsome." I cautioned her and she left.'

Brian Hobbs tut-tutted but Harry Andrews couldn't contain his mirth. David looked at him sternly.

'I expect my officers to set some sort of example, Harry.'

Harry grinned broadly. 'Yes. sir. Sorry, sir.'

'Is that the lot, Col?'

'The Rileys were very protective of one another and very quiet. They didn't talk in front of me.'

'Good. All right, Col, thanks. You can get away now.'

'Thank you, sir.'

David turned to me. 'Wondering why I let you stay?'

'Sort of.'

'I've told you before, you're an excellent observer but you don't always realize what you know. You've heard the various versions of the evening. Think back, Micky, and see if anything doesn't fit. You know these people. Someone knew Maddy Grey was there, someone went over to her during the evening, someone killed her. Therefore, someone had taken the ice pick either on the spur of the moment or earlier, to await their chance. If anything comes to you, I'll be at the station. Probably all night, so you won't be disturbing me.'

'Will you let me know how you get on?'

'As much as I can—if I feel it's appropriate.'

'Does it have to be one of these people?' I asked unhappily.

'It rather points that way. There were two necessary ingredients. One, knowledge of where the deceased was sitting and two, enough of a reason to be rid of her. Any one of the general public might have known where she was but why would they want to kill her?'

I shrugged. My brain felt numb. David stood up. 'Go home, Micky, sleep on it. Perhaps something will slot into place.'

CHAPTER 23

I ran the Capri into my parking space outside No. 18 and sat for a moment staring across the dark, shadowed park opposite. A mopoke called from the fig tree, annoyed at having the silence disturbed, and the harsh chatter of a possum sounded somewhere in the park.

The sky was dark and moonless. The few visible stars bright enough not to be intimidated by the city's neon glowed coldly above me. I shivered and slowly locked the car door. I felt heavy with exhaustion but knew I wouldn't sleep. Sick at heart, I trod up the front steps and let myself into the flats.

It was very quiet. A thin sliver of light showed under the door of No. 3 and as I climbed the stairs I could hear a thread of soothing flute music. I hesitated, then knocked gently.

The door opened and Al Wang's good-humoured face looked out. 'Michael! What has happened? An accident of some sort? Come inside.'

'Are you busy?' The sweet scent of incense hung in the air.

'No, I am merely entertaining a guest.'

'Oh! Well, I won't disturb you.'

'My dear Michael, my guest is well known to you.' He took my arm. 'You look all in, my friend.'

He drew me into the room. I don't know what it is but Al's place is like balm to the spirits. Simple, uncluttered, its soft colours restful to the eyes. Across the room Al's guest sat on a cushion on the floor. She gave me a baleful stare and deliberately turned her back to me and began to wash herself.

'Carnie!' I exclaimed guiltily. 'Oh God, I forgot about you, Princess.'

'You've been gone for a long time,' Al said without rancour. 'I found her crying at your door and invited her down.'

'Thanks, Al. I left her outside. I should have been home hours ago.'

'But you were delayed? Your face tells it all. Sit down and relax. I will make some Chinese tea and you will tell us what has happened. Perhaps then Carnation will forgive you.'

I sat back in a low bean-bag chair and sipped the fragrant, steaming tea, feeling my tension slipping away. The soft meditation music seemed to absorb my mind and my thoughts began to slow down. Al settled himself on the floor next to me.

'Now, tell me what has disturbed you, my friend.'

I told him, trying to keep my voice from shaking. I felt numb as the shock began to set in. Al watched me with concern but didn't interrupt. I felt I was talking to myself. At some stage Carnie gave a sudden ripple and stepped daintily into my lap, kneading it to suit herself. I was grateful for her soft warmth under my fingers as she purred herself to sleep. When I'd finished Al's moon face was grave.

'This is very distressing, Michael.'

'I've gone over and over it. I've worked out the times pretty exactly for everyone and I just can't believe any of them did it—and yet I'm pretty sure David has a clear suspect already.'

'Your friend Don Riley?'

'I think—I'm not sure it's Don but I know David. He's working to a plan already. He started off by getting everyone to tell their whole view of events as they saw them but in the end he was only going for odd points.'

'The Inspector is a very clever man. He will find out the

truth. As he says, it must have been someone who wished
her dead, who knew she was in the garden and who visited
the drinks table for the ice pick. Who is the person who fits
this description?'

I shrugged. The strange inertia I'd been feeling was dropping away and my interest stirred.

'The Rileys were in trouble because of the loss of the
Kids' World franchise and Don and Fiona had the extra
worry over Maddy's threat to close them down. Gillian Fry
was angry about her book being stopped by Maddy. Jessica
Savage had a lawsuit to fight—but I really don't see her
doing murder. It's all in the line of business for her. Gwen
Bright was unhappy about Maddy dropping her, but honestly, Al, she wouldn't have done it. She was hypnotized
by Maddy. Besotted by her.'

'A dangerous state. She might kill to be free of her. What
about the producer, Tony Ridgeway?'

'Not a chance. Maddy annoyed the hell out of him but
he was expert at handling her and he needed her for the
show. He was planning to get her into a clinic and straightened out.'

'Her daughter? Little Angela, whom she brutalized and
was sending away from her lover?'

'Hang on, Al, they're not lovers.'

'Not physically, perhaps. Love does not only consist of
sexual activity. They are lovers in their hearts.'

'All right, but I don't know if she'd told Angela her plans
—anyway, it's ridiculous. Angie protected Maddy. She was
more like Maddy's mother at times.'

'Mr West? Madeline Grey sacked him from her show and
presumably his career would suffer. Also, he was to be
stopped from seeing Angela.'

I shook my head. 'Maddy was going to get him in some
series down south. And he'd never cause Angela that sort
of grief.'

'How grieved was she? You told me she was very calm

—unnaturally so. She made no attempt to wake her mother —perhaps she already knew she was dead. She did not try to run to her when told the terrible news.'

'Oh, come on!' I started, but Al held up his hand.

'Michael, listen to me. You are too close. Your mind is confused by loyalties and emotions. You like this one, you don't like that one. Now I don't know these people. I am therefore unbiased and I see what may not be obvious to you.'

'Well, it's a moot point anyway, because we know she was alive after Angela saw her.'

'Perhaps,' Al said maddeningly. 'What if one of these people is lying?'

'Why on earth would they lie?'

He gave me his most irritatingly inscrutable smile. 'Why indeed?'

I toyed with Carnie's fur. 'OK, you asked who could have got the ice pick? Tony brought Maddy down and got her a drink. If the pick was on the table he could have got it and killed Maddy when he went back to her, but Gwen said she was alive later. And he'd hardly have dosed her with sleeping tablets if he'd meant to kill her anyway. According to Bobby, Gwen had been at the table and could have taken the pick when she went to Maddy, but Bobby, who saw her next, said she was alive and muttering in her sleep. Bobby had also been at the drinks table, so Jessica says, just before he went to Maddy. He could have killed her, but Angela said she was asleep and snoring—not much doubt that she was alive then. No one said they saw Angie at the table. She seems to have checked with Tony, then gone straight to Maddy after Bobby had left. Could she have got the ice pick? Probably not. If she had, Jessica would have noticed and said something. However, Fiona was at the table and she went over to Maddy. She says Maddy was asleep. I don't think she could have had the ice pick because, before then, she and Don had been looking for it and Fi had to go upstairs for the hammer. Unless Fi hid the pick and pretended it had gone missing earlier to throw suspicion on to someone else. I've known Fi for years and I just don't believe it. She's thoroughly nice and very sensible. The other person, is, of course, Don, who moved around with a tray and could have gone over to Maddy. He also could have hidden the ice pick earlier and said it was missing to throw suspicion on one of the others. Who have I missed out?'

Al frowned. 'Miss Fry and Miss Savage, I think. You said Miss Fry was drinking after fighting with the deceased.'

'Don't do that,' I snapped irritably. 'You sound like David Reeves. Maddy has a name.'

He smiled gently. 'Yes, but she is not using her body any more. However, if it discomforts you, I will call her Maddy, as you do.'

'Sorry, Al,' I said sheepishly. 'I'm a bit tired. Don't forget Gillian reckoned she didn't know Maddy came downstairs. Could she have taken the pick with the idea of going back up to the office? And if so, why didn't she go upstairs again? It doesn't work for Jess, either. She admits she went down for a drink but that was early. She couldn't have known Maddy wouldn't do the launch and not be in the gazebo most of the evening, then socializing like the others. Anyway, I don't.think she had enough motive. She was getting all the revenge she wanted in her own way.'

'Miss Fry could have seen Maddy coming down. You only have her word for it that she did not notice.'

'True, but nobody saw her go over to the corner—no one who was interviewed, anyway. Again, Jess would have said. Then there's Frank. He went to the drinks table but no one saw him near Maddy. I did get the impression he didn't like her, but that's hardly a motive for murder. If we all went around bumping off people we didn't like . . .'

'There would be a drastic reduction in the Earth's population. I agree. However, the Inspector has many more

people to interview. Perhaps much more will be discovered.'
Al refilled our cups and looked thoughtfully at me. 'So,
unless the police find otherwise, we know who had reason
to hate her, and who visited the drinks table. Now, which
of these knew she was in the garden?'

'Tony, Gwen, Angela, Bobby, myself, of course, John
Riley, Fiona and possibly Don, but we don't know and he
says not—and I'm inclined to believe him.'

'You, my friend, are inclined to believe everyone. We are
making progress. Can you think of any other who might
have wished for her death?'

'I'd been almost wishing for it myself,' I said grimly, 'but
only because she'd been making so many people miserable.
There might have been scores of others.'

'But they were not at your book launch. What of those
you have already named?'

'They'd all been exasperated by her, angered, worried,
upset by her—and, yes, perhaps even wished her dead—
but it's a big leap from idly thinking to actually doing.
Wishing doesn't do any harm and it certainly relieves the
tension, but I can't see any of them as a killer.'

'No, you can't, and yet the lady is dead. You said the
Rileys—John and Barbara because of the franchise, Don
and Fiona for the added reason for her threat to close the
shop. Her death has been a blessing for them. Yes,' he
mused, 'that is how it should be looked at. Who is now very
much better off?'

'Jessica?' I suggested.

'Is she? Miss Savage has lost a well loved opponent and
the publicity of a court case which, no doubt, she would
have relished. Think of the new readers she would gain.'

'That's a funny thing to say,' I protested. 'She certainly
didn't love Maddy.'

'No? I read her column, you know. She is witty and
entertaining. I agree with her statement. She will be lost
without Madeline Grey. Now she will have no one outside

herself to attack for the loss of Morgan Grey and she will most likely be forced to look into herself and face what she has denied for so long. A lonely and painful journey. So much easier to have an outside focus for guilt and anger.'

I was silent. Al was right. Jessica had looked a lonely, lost woman under her cool sarcasm.

Al's face was serene. 'Miss Bright is better off. She is rid of a virago who chained her to herself through Miss Bright's own weakness and fear of being alone. She is free of the uncertainty of Madeline Grey's erratic behaviour, of her temper, of the retribution she would certainly seek for Miss Bright's betrayal of her with her daughter. We only have her word that Maddy would have taken her back and that she loved Maddy so much. Again, things are not always what they appear on the surface. She may have hated her for years and locked her feelings deep inside her.'

'What about Frank?' I was sceptical. 'I suppose he was seething with passionate hate as well?'

'No.' Al gave that knowing smile. 'Passion, perhaps, or why was he so distressed by her death? And remember their terrible quarrel only the day before.'

'Look, you're really fantasizing now. Frank's a very hap- pily married man, devoted to his wife, and he hardly knew Maddy—and he didn't like her that much. I reckon Tracey must have been exaggerating—over-dramatizing what she heard. Frank probably went to pieces because he's under pressure at the studio. He wants to make the new time slots work, he's got a career move to decide—and because he's a nice, sensitive bloke and violent murder sickens him. I felt pretty sick myself. And don't forget, he found the body. That's disturbing enough.'

'Michael, I'm not going to try to convince you. I suggest you look at Mr Young very carefully. His timing is sugges- tive of quite a different case.'

'Eh? What on earth are you on about?'

'No, I will say no more. Let us move to Miss Fry.'

'Well, there I have to agree with you,' I said reluctantly. 'Gilly is much better off. She can get *City Tribe* published, Angela's out of trouble, which she really was concerned about, and it's all worked out very well for her. But *Gilly*? She wouldn't have the nerve.'

'She had the nerve to confront her tormenter earlier.'

'You choose the oddest way of saying things,' I told him.

'Was she not tormented?'

'Yes. Yes, she was.'

'And now not? We do not accuse here, we merely speculate. The Inspector has asked you to think it all through. Now, the young Romeo and Juliet, Angela Grey and Bobby West. Their lot has certainly improved. Romeo is free to court his lady in due course, he is also free of an embarrassing reminder of a past indiscretion, a domineering, clinging woman and, presumably, he will now take the senior role in the show he loves. Juliet is also free—to pursue her life and career without interference and with much support from Mr Ridgeway, I gather. Free of abuse, both verbal and physical, and free to love without fear of discovery or retribution. A highly desirable position.'

'She was devastated,' I said curtly. 'She loved Maddy, in spite of her mother's behaviour. She looked after her.'

'And yet, as I have pointed out, she made no move at all to help her.'

'She was badly shocked, Al. It takes people in different ways.

'So it does, and you're saying I should know that? You are very right to say it. Now we have Mr Ridgeway.'

'He hasn't gained anything,' I said, 'except an awful lot of problems. He's lost a star—and she was a big name, Al, and popular nationwide. He's got to save the show, deal with all the flak and adverse publicity. He looked really put out by the whole thing. He must have been worried as hell all evening, you could see it in his face at the end. In his own way I think he liked Maddy. He tolerated an awful lot from her. I think he always remembered the happy times when he started with *Kids' World*. He and Morgan and Maddy were inseparable. She was really fun in those days. Happy and warm-hearted and incredible to look at. You've got no idea. I probably would've fallen for her myself, except—'

'Except?' Al prompted.

It was my turn to frown. 'I never quite trusted her,' I said slowly. 'I felt there was something unstable about her even then. Anyway, Morgan and I were mates.'

'Your good instincts didn't let you down. Trust them now.' He leaned towards me. 'Have you thought that there may not be just one murderer, but two?'

I looked at him. 'Two?' I repeated stupidly.

'The marks on Madeline Grey's throat. It is not very likely that someone strangled her, then stabbed her. It seems more probable that she was strangled by one, then stabbed by another.'

I suddenly remembered John Riley's voice and the look of despair on his face. He'd said, 'I'd like to strangle her.' It was so ludicrous I quickly banished the thought and shook my head. My brain felt numb. There was another awful possibility. I felt the words being wrung out of me.

'Or that the murderer had an accomplice and it was done deliberately to avert suspicion and confuse the police.'

I had a sudden sick picture of Bobby and Angela— Bobby strangling Maddy and Angela stabbing her immediately afterwards. Was that why David had questioned Bobby so persistently, asking if he was sure there was nothing else he wanted to say? And he'd made that cryptic remark about them being a devoted pair. Then, what if Don and Fiona had plotted Maddy's death as they worked together and pretended the ice pick was already gone?

Al suddenly unfolded himself and stood up. 'You need your bed, Michael. Think about it. Somehow I feel the answer is here now. But sleep on it first.'

I took Carnie home. I felt drained. I tried to go back once again over what I'd seen from the gazebo but the people began to shift and spin in my mind, becoming confused and jumbled, and I fell soundly asleep.

CHAPTER 24

Carnie woke me by sitting on my chest and yowling, her claws like needles in my skin. I looked at her stupidly for a moment, then realized I was in pain and yelled, pushing her off on to the bed. She gave me a smug look and tidied her whiskers. I pulled myself up and padded downstairs. 'About time!' my flatmate told me and got to the kitchen first, leaping gracefully on to the sink to bat the water as I filled the jug.

We'd settled down to our respective breakfasts when the phone began. It took a few moments for the news to sink in that Maddy's death was splashed all over the front page of Jessica's paper and that I was in urgent demand for a comment, an interview, anything! As well as the media, shocked friends and launch guests rang to express concern, horror, interest and blatant curiosity. After an hour of floundering through various conversations I switched over to the answering machine, my new toy, and let it earn its keep.

As I was deciding what to do next there was a knock at the door.

'David! What on earth . . . !'

'I was on my way to the station.' He looked grave. 'I thought you'd better hear this from me.'

My stomach sank. 'Come in. Have you made an arrest?'

'No, it's not that.' He settled himself on the sofa and tickled Carnie's chin, which she loves. 'It seems Miss Bright killed herself last night.'

'Oh no!' I sat down, shocked. 'Don't tell me it was her after all.'

'It certainly looks like it. She left a suicide note asking to be forgiven, supposedly went to the garage and turned on the car engine. She died of carbon monoxide poisoning. I thought you'd rather hear it from me in person.'

'You couldn't have got through on the phone, anyway, it's been on the go all morning.' My mind was grasping at anything mundane in order not to have to think about poor, shattered Gwen, dying like that.

'Yes, I'm afraid Miss Savage has caused you some problems. Don't worry, it'll all die down now.

'Tell me everything, David.'

'Miss Bright took a taxi to the Greys' house to pick up her car. She'd left it there earlier and come to the launch with the Ridgeways, as you know. The taxi-driver says she was very upset and seemed in a state of shock. He offered to take her to her house instead and warned her against driving in her condition. She said she hadn't far to go and he waited until she drove away to check she was OK.'

'Nice of him,' I commented.

'Apparently she got home, made herself a mug of cocoa and went to bed. The half-empty cup was on her bedside table. She was found in her nightdress, dressing-gown and slippers. The idea is that she was overcome by guilt, wrote her letter, then killed herself. Her head was lying on her pillow,' he said inconsequentially. 'It's a well-known habit with suicides, to make themselves as comfortable as possible. You wouldn't think it mattered. Her body was right by the exhaust pipe and her garage is well built. A good, close-fitting door.' He stopped, seeing the horror in my face.

'Poor Gwen. So she really did kill Maddy.' I shook my head. It was hard to believe.

'Well, it looks that way.' David reached into his pocket and brought out a paper encased in a plastic bag.

'"Please forgive me,"' he read. '"I didn't mean to do it.

I feel terrible and I can't go on any more. It was no one else's fault, just mine. I'm deeply sorry for all the trouble I've caused. I'd rather die than live like this." It's signed "Gwen."'

I cleared my throat. Nothing occurred to me to say. Carnie patted David's hand, annoyed to have lost his attention.

'It doesn't explain everything,' he said, 'but it's her writing all right, and she was blaming herself last night. I knew she wasn't telling us the truth. After a while you get to know. I thought she must have seen someone kill Mrs Grey. Still, if she did it, it would fit the facts as we know them.'

We sat for a moment in silence, then David said, 'You knew the Greys from the start. I expect you've got photographs? I'd like to see Morgan Grey.'

I got up and went to the bookshelf, taking down a photograph album. It was curiously soothing to see Morgan and Maddy still alive and smiling out from the pages.

'That's their wedding, there's Gwen as the head bridesmaid. I was best man.'

'A handsome couple.' David seemed absorbed by the scene.

'Morgan always was a distinguished-looking man. You can see how beautiful Maddy was. Ethereal and so fair—like an angel.'

'I begin to understand.' David continued to pore over the album. When he looked up again he smiled absently. 'Could I take this one with me?'

'Be my guest.' It was a casual snapshot of Morgan and Maddy, dark head and fair together at some function, looking very much in love.

'Thanks, Micky. I'll be on my way. One last thing.' He disengaged Carnie's reluctant paw and stood up. 'Do you know if Mrs Grey might have hit Miss Bright in a moment of temper? Before the Ridgeways arrived to collect them yesterday evening, for instance?'

I stared at him. 'Good God, I can't imagine—but then,

she hit Angela and I never knew. It's possible. What makes you think . . . ?'

'There was a nasty contusion on Miss Bright's temple, hidden by her hair. She might have had an accident, of course. It was just a thought.'

I saw David off in a daze, grateful that he'd thought to tell me about Gwen himself. Then I rang the Ridgeways.

'Yes, please come around,' Becky said. 'We're all here.'

She welcomed me at the door. 'Isn't it awful?' she said. 'The police rang us earlier and they've been around questioning us all again. The two sergeants from last night.' She ushered me into the living-room where Tony was pouring himself a drink.

'It's too early, but what the hell! One for you, Micky?'

'I'd rather a coffee,' I said and Becky nodded. 'I was just making it when you arrived. Sit down, Micky. I won't be a moment.'

'Well, this is a turn-up for the books,' Tony said. 'Who'd have thought Gwenny had it in her?'

'Who found her?' I'd meant to ask David but had been too numb with shock.

'Next-door neighbour. She gets the paper delivered. Saw the story about Maddy and rushed next door. Found the front door unlocked and saw the note Gwenny left. She couldn't find her and finally thought of the garage. Nasty shock.'

'Horrible!' I shuddered.

Becky brought in a tray and poured coffee. 'Well, at least it's all over quickly,' she said. 'Now we can get our lives back to normal. Poor Angela was terribly upset. She's lying down.'

'And it'll get the police off our backs,' Tony said brusquely. 'They were here earlier, still asking questions about our relationship with Maddy and going over our statements of last night even though Gwenny confessed. Wanted all the little details. Even how I got my sleeve wet!

Can you imagine? You'd think they'd have better things to
do.'

'Frank mentioned it, but only in passing,' I told him. 'He
said you got a drink and your sleeve was wet. He noticed
because you were shaking it.'

'Cuff, not sleeve,' he said crossly. 'Frank should mind his
bloody business. I got myself a punch and went to put ice
in it but all I found was slush in the bottom. I fished around
for some bigger chunks and went in deeper than I thought.
It was bloody uncomfortable.'

'Never mind,' Becky said soothingly, 'it'll be all over
soon.' She poured him a coffee. 'Try this. It's hard for
Tony,' she said to me. 'He's got to reschedule the shooting
and find someone to replace Maddy. They've got a few
days in the can, which is a blessing. We've been inundated
by callers as well—sensation-seekers, mostly. We've had to
put the answering machine on. We got tired of saying "no
comment" and "a press statement will be released later
today." Darling,' she said to Tony, 'aren't you going to be
late?'

'Christ!' Tony looked at the clock. 'Thanks, Becky.' He
turned to me. 'Sorry to run out on you, Micky, I've got to
get up to the studio. Listen, mate, we've still got an issue
here. Now things have changed, I've been hoping there's
at least one bright spot and you'll reconsider Winifred for
Kids' World. Last night's given us a lot of publicity.'

As Tony went out Becky smiled at me. 'Sorry, Micky,
it's just his way. He's still got to find ways to keep the show
going. You can't blame him for seeing opportunities, it's
his job. He's very sorry about Maddy.' She poured herself
another cup. 'In a way, I am too, although I never liked
her. She was always having digs at me, trying to give the
impression that she and Tony had little secrets I didn't
know about—you know the way she was. Putting on airs
to be interesting.' She put down her cup and her hands
were shaking. Coffee slopped into the saucer.

'Bother! Look at me, all nerves. I didn't get much sleep last night. None of us did. Tony was like a rag this morning. Angela was very restless, so I slept in her room. It was Tony's idea, bless him. He was worried she might need me in the night. When I did get to sleep I was woken up a couple of times by cars on the road outside. You know how every noise seems extra loud when you're over-tired. And, just as we'd got to bed, Jasmine rang, having a fit because Frank hadn't come home. She'd rung the channel, of course, only to find he hadn't been there. She tried to raise the shop but everyone must have left by then. She even rang the police! Anyway, as she was talking to me, Frank arrived home. It must have been after midnight. We'd put Angela to bed and Tony and I had stayed up talking—and taking Dr Edgely's advice—a couple of stiff drinks.' She stopped and looked worried. 'Micky, Maddy never hit Gwen about, did she?'

'Not that I know of. Did the police ask you, too?'

'Yes, I thought it was a bit odd. They didn't say why they wanted to know. I couldn't tell them but I couldn't discount it either. She was pretty mad with Gwen.'

Angela appeared at the door, her face tearstained. She said, 'Hello, Micky,' and went to sit by Becky.

'Are you all right, Angel?' I asked anxiously.

'Yes, thank you.' She sounded exhausted. 'Is that coffee fresh, Becky? May I have some?'

'I'll make another pot.' Becky took the tray out.

'Angel, I'm more sorry than I can say,' I began, but she interrupted me.

'I liked Gwen.' Her voice was shaky. 'She really did try to help me. She was sorry for me and encouraged me. She was going to be my agent, did you know? She said Dad had arranged something and Mum couldn't stop me.' She wiped her eyes. 'Mum was so—so mean to Gwen sometimes but Gwen stood by her and supported her. When Mum sacked her Gwen just wanted to die. She sent Mum a lovely bunch

of flowers with a note. Mum just laughed and said Gwen
was pathetic and it served her right. She showed the note
to Tony and had a real giggle over it. It wasn't fair. Gwen
always took on all the guilt and all the blame. It must have
all got to her in the end. I wish—I wish she'd been able to
let Mum go—but nobody could.'

'I know.' I couldn't think of any way to comfort her. I
stayed for a while longer then left, feeling totally in-
adequate.

CHAPTER 25

As I entered No. 18, Monica pounced on me.

'Oh, Micky, is it true? That lovely woman murdered at
your book launch? You poor love.'

I gave her a brief outline and escaped up the stairs. Once
again Al Wang opened his door to me.

'Good, I hoped you would look in.' He smiled gently.
'I've seen the paper.'

'Gwen Bright did it!' I blurted out, and told him.

'Ah!' He nodded several times, looking more inscrutable
than ever. 'Did she admit to the stabbing or the strangulation?'

'Bloody hell!' I stared at him.

'It would be most interesting to find out.'

'The note just said she was sorry and she was totally to
blame, no one else.'

'Was she saying she first tried to strangle Mrs Grey and
then stabbed her? Why would she have done that?'

'That must have been what David meant when he said
some things were unexplained but it fitted the facts as they
knew them.'

'I have been thinking about those facts myself. The man
who discovered the body, what exactly did he say again?'

I repeated Frank's words as well as I could remember them.

Al looked unusually serious. 'I wonder when Miss Bright committed the murder.'

'It must have been after Fiona saw Maddy,' I said slowly. 'That was about ten past seven. I worked out how long it would take everyone to make their moves. I'd say between ten past and a quarter past seven. Gwen must have waited at the top of the garden and slipped back to Maddy under cover of the confusion of everyone leaving. She could have, easily, then gone back and come up with me later.'

'I thought you said someone saw Miss Bright moving down the garden.'

'Jessica said she'd hung around Tony for a while and then "pushed off". She didn't say where. Oh, I remember —Frank Young said she went back down the garden, but he might have been wrong. It's possible that he only saw her going in that direction or Gwen moved in front of someone and waited there. Frank was pretty distracted himself. He didn't get home until after midnight last night and his wife had been ringing around in a panic to find him.'

Al's face was grave. 'Is that so?' He looked at his watch. 'I am due at my clinic. Micky, something is wrong here. I have a very bad feeling about all this. Please think over our conversation and you'll see what I say is true. I am deeply concerned that there may be more deaths. I said last night someone might be lying.'

Although I tried, Al wouldn't be drawn. He went off down the stairs, leaving me to wonder what he meant. I prowled restlessly around my flat and eventually thought to check my messages. I ran through the tape. All the usual stuff, except for one. A familiar voice, pleasantly deep, but now taut with worry.

'Micky? Frank Young. Would you give me a call as soon as you can? At home on—' he gave the number—'or at the studio after lunch. It's urgent. Thanks.'

I dialled his home number. He must have been sitting on the phone, he answered it so promptly.

'What's the trouble, Frank?'

'I need to talk to you. The police rang earlier. Can you come up to the studio this afternoon? Only I don't want Jasmine to know.' He dropped to an urgent undertone. 'Please. I think I'm going to need help.'

We made a time and I rang off, my curiosity thoroughly aroused. I thought about lunch but didn't feel like making anything. Even a sandwich would have been too much effort. In the end I put Carnie out the back door to amuse herself and went to Henri's.

'Micky, bad news,' he greeted me. 'Everyone's talking about it. Come and sit down. I'll give you an alcove and if you sit with your back to the room you'll be all right.'

'Eh?' I was startled.

'Don't you know? You're a celebrity, your face in the paper. I'll show you.' He reached behind the servery counter and produced Jessica's tabloid. I sat down weakly.

'It's very sad about the Rileys having business troubles,' Henri said as he prepared the table. 'It's no good for small businesses any more. Look at us. We're struggling these days. Too many shops in the arcade are going broke, so we don't get the flow of customers we used to. Sometimes the place is deserted. I want to move to a more central location.'

'Jessica's even given you a mention,' I said absently.

'Sure, she said she dined here, so we'll be a nine days' wonder, then back to the way we were. Riley's, too. People will flock there for the thrill of it for a few weeks but it won't help in the long run. She says in there Maddy Grey was going to send them broke. Hints it was good for them that she died when she did.'

'Hell! That's nasty.' I handed him back the paper.

'But true, no?' I admitted it. 'Well, Micky, what will you have today?'

I ate Henri's good food, turning my conversation with Al

over in my mind. I was floundering around with everyone's stories jostling together and nothing becoming clear at all. I felt somehow I had the answer but it was eluding me. Everything was so contradictory. Maddy was snoring and she wasn't, she was stabbed but she was strangled, Frank was distressed but didn't like Maddy, he'd left to go home but he hadn't arrived there, and—my mind went off at a tangent—why did he want to see me so urgently? Gwen loved Maddy but killed her and admitted it for all the world to see. I went over the note in my mind again. Angela's sad voice came back to me, 'I wish she'd been able to let Mum go, but nobody could.' No, nobody could and that was the tragedy of it. And yet, I told myself, Bobby had. It was Maddy who wouldn't let him go. She'd tried to bind him to her, making suggestive remarks, alienating him. Just like —I stared at the wine glass in front of me. Suddenly I pushed back my chair.

'That's Michael Douglas, the author,' a voice said, and I hastily paid Henri and bolted.

The gate-keeper rang through to the studio and waved me on to the visitors' car park. I found a space for the Capri by the wire fence which segregated the visitors from the staff parking area. Tony Ridgeway's sky blue Jaguar was there next to Bobby West's silver Porsche. *Kids' World* had been good to them both.

I made my way through the gardens and up to reception. Frank Young came down himself and took me up to the second floor where the news teams had their offices.

'What a tragic thing,' he said, but his mind was elsewhere. 'I wouldn't have believed it of Gwen but Maddy was certainly being very hard on her. This way, Micky.' He led the way into a small interview room and closed the door. 'It's soundproof,' he said as the outside noise cut off suddenly. 'I wanted to be private.'

Beyond the thick glass window news reporters came and

went, phones rang frantically, groups huddled, planning the news broadcasts.

'What's this about?' I took the chair Frank was indicating and he drew up another for himself. He didn't look in much better shape than he had at Riley's.

'Micky, I need your help,' he said abruptly. 'The thing is, it's a personal matter and it can't go any further.'

'Of course not,' I said hastily. 'Look, are you sure this is my business?'

'I was having an affair with Maddy,' he said and stopped me in my tracks. 'I was the man she dropped West for. It was two years ago in the New Year. I'd just joined the studio. I started with her and then decided I couldn't go on because of Jasmine and the children. I told Maddy I wanted to end it.' He was white to the lips. 'She refused to let go. She threatened to tell Jasmine everything. I tried to get away from her, I swear I did, but I—it was like a nightmare.'

He stopped and buried his face in his hands. I was stunned. I thought stupidly: I already knew this, in the back of my mind. I said gently, 'You were the newsreader Jessica was talking about in her column.' Suddenly it was so obvious; the way Maddy had treated him at her party, just the way she behaved to Bobby, teasing him, cajoling him, trying to hang on to him, refusing to let go. I'd heard a lot about how men couldn't leave Maddy but it suddenly occurred to me that it was just the opposite. She was the one who wouldn't let go, who clung on desperately, afraid of being left alone. Jessica had hinted as much and Bobby had said even though she'd broken it off, she never stopped trying to hold on to him.

Frank raised his head. 'I almost hated her at times, then I'd feel the magic of her and I was like a boy in love. I was sick with wanting her and yet at the same time I knew I had to get free of her or she'd destroy me.'

'That's why you changed your times,' I said. 'The six

o'clock news is prime time and yet you deliberately asked for a later slot. I wondered about that. It was to avoid Maddy. Then, you said you were planning a career move but you suddenly changed your mind—as soon as Maddy was dead.'

Frank nodded. 'You're right. My God, I've been ill with all of this. I'd just never met anyone like Maddy. Jasmine suddenly seemed so ordinary—dull and commonplace—beside her. I fell hook, line and sinker. She sucked me in so fast I couldn't believe it. Then later,' he said bleakly, 'later I came to my senses. It wasn't love. I never really loved her. I was infatuated, but by then I couldn't get away. Maddy got hysterical if I suggested a break. Once she tried to kill herself, or so she said, after I told her it was all off. I was terrified she'd try it again. Finally Jasmine realized something was wrong. I told her it was pressure of work. She suggested the change. I asked Russell before he went on holiday and spoke to the producers. Then Maddy panicked. She started threatening me. If I didn't see her again she'd tell Jasmine, go to the papers, ruin my marriage. I'm in love with my wife, deeply so. I can't explain the thing with Maddy but I knew it would pass.'

'Frank,' I broke in, 'why are you telling me all this? What do you want me to do?'

'The police called. I told you. They asked all sorts of questions about last night, about the launch and where I went afterwards. They're on their way up here now. They want to talk to me.' He gave me a worried look. 'They can't think I did it—they've got Gwen's confession. They seem to think I had something to do with both deaths. For God's sake, I don't want this to get back to Jasmine. The Inspector's a friend of yours. Get him to keep me out of it, please!'

'I'll try,' I said, 'but it rather depends how deep you're in it, Frank.'

CHAPTER 26

I watched Frank, my mind racing. He had risen and was pacing about, much as I'd been doing earlier, but the small room didn't offer much scope for him to work off his anxiety and he sat down again, his face taut.

I hesitated, wondering if I should voice the thought which was growing in my head. My grandmother used to say, 'A trouble shared is a trouble halved,' but Frank didn't need any more troubles, even half a one. Eventually I spoke, feeling awkward and a little stupid.

'Frank, look, it's just an idea a friend and I talked over but it's possible there were two attempts on Maddy's life.'

He stared blankly at me while I explained.

'So you see,' I finished, 'even if Gwen stabbed Maddy, it looks as if someone had already attempted to strangle her and thought they'd succeeded. The police may be looking for a second suspect, or an accomplice.'

'And they think it was me?'

'Well, you did go to the drinks table and you could have taken the ice pick, perhaps to give to Gwen. They've only your word for it that you didn't go to Maddy and it did seem as if you were hanging around looking out for her. After what you've told me, I'd have thought you wouldn't want to be anywhere near her.'

His voice was grim. 'I was keeping close to her because she told me she was going to use her speech to announce that we were lovers.'

'Good God!' I shuddered, imagining the scene, horrified to find myself profoundly thankful someone had stopped her.

'Exactly. So you see, I had to stay close to her. I didn't know what I was going to do—I didn't think that far.

However, I promise you, I didn't stab her or try to strangle her. I couldn't. For one thing, violence always makes me ill—' he flushed—'ever since I was a kid. My father was a violent man. He used to beat the hell out of cane toads with a shovel and I'd throw up. He hated that. Thought I was queer or something. When I went into television he was sure of it.' His face relaxed into a half smile. 'I think he still wonders if I fathered my children.'

I suddenly thought about the conversation Tracey had overheard. Maddy had threatened to tell the truth about Frank and Morgan Grey. Was it possible . . . I shook myself guiltily. Frank's story had brought a twinge of empathy. He was telling me the story of my own childhood. Physical violence was never my sport either and I failed my father's expectations dismally. He thinks all writers are cissies and despairs of me to this day.

Frank interrupted my thoughts. 'God, what am I going to do? I don't understand why they'd think it was me. And what can it matter where I was last night?'

Suddenly I knew and my certainty made me cringe inside.

'What is it?' Frank was watching my face. 'It's just a guess,' I admitted, 'but I'll bet I'm right. Gwen didn't commit suicide. She's been murdered, Frank.' He gave an exclamation of disbelief, but I hurried on. 'David Reeves wasn't happy about Gwen's confession. Her note didn't actually say, "I killed her." It was rather vague. If it wasn't suicide, then someone killed her because she saw who killed Maddy. When you left Riley's you were supposed to be going straight home only you didn't get there until after midnight, which is a hell of a long time unless you—er—detoured by Gwen's place—you see?'

He was a worried man. 'I didn't see who killed Maddy,' he snapped. 'I didn't go near Gwen's last night.' Then he shrugged and dropped his voice. 'I felt ill,' he said, 'I knew if I went home Jasmine would guess everything. I must

have had guilt written all over my face. I live in New Farm
and I went to New Farm Park and sat by the river. It was
so peaceful, just one or two people about, and the scent of
the roses was beautiful. I stayed there breathing it all in
until I thought I could go home and act normally. Of course
I'd lost track of the time, so Jasmine found out I wasn't at
the studio at all. I told her the police had held me up. She
believed me. I wouldn't hurt her for anything, Micky.'

'Did anyone see you at the park?'

'I don't know. People may have driven past but I didn't
notice. Anyway, you know what that place is like.' He
smiled slightly. 'At that hour they'd only notice each other.'

'Never mind, the police will make inquiries and maybe
someone did see you who'll confirm your story.'

'Speak for me, Micky,' he said urgently. 'With the
Inspector. Tell him I didn't do it—couldn't do it.'

'There's something else,' I said quietly. 'It isn't looking
good for you, Frank. You see, Maddy's secretary overheard
you having what she called a "colossal row" with Maddy
on Sunday night. She told Gwen and Gwen told the Inspector. You could have killed Maddy and then Gwen, to shut
her up in case she told anyone.'

'What?' He was startled. 'No, that's not true.'

'Tracey heard you,' I persisted. 'You were fighting about
Maddy's husband, Morgan. I didn't know you knew him.
Something about if you didn't do what she wanted she'd
tell the truth about you and Morgan and it would ruin your
marriage.' I stopped, seeing his look of blank amazement.

'It just isn't true,' he repeated. 'How could Tracey say
that? I didn't have a row with Maddy and I never knew
Morgan Grey. I don't know what you're talking about.'

'You had an appointment with Maddy on Sunday night,'
I told him. 'It was in her diary.'

His shoulders sagged. 'Yes, that's right. Maddy wanted
me to go and see her. She knew I was trying to break with
her. She was frightened because I'd avoided her for weeks.

She threatened to tell Jasmine everything if I didn't go.'

'So you did have a fight with her.'

'No!' His head snapped back, his eyes blazing. 'I didn't keep the appointment. I never went near her that night. I decided once and for all to be a man and not give in to her, so I called her bluff. I didn't turn up.'

'You didn't go at all?' I said slowly.

'No, I didn't, so I don't know what Tracey thought she heard, but it wasn't me.'

There was a tap on the door and a girl looked in, her expression betraying her interest.

'Frank, sorry to interrupt, but the police are here. They want to talk to you.'

Frank stood up and squared his shoulders. He gave me a brief smile. 'Well, at least I'm prepared for them. Thanks for coming, Micky. I don't suppose there's anything you can do now.'

I watched him walk across the newsroom under the curious gaze of the staff, to where Harry Andrews was waiting for him.

A few minutes later I opened the door to Tony's suite.

CHAPTER 27

Karen Blair, looking subdued in a grey suit and lavender blouse, gave me a brief smile and continued to deal with the frantically ringing phone. I sat down and flicked through a magazine until there was a lull.

'Sorry about that, Mr Douglas, it's been crazy all day.' Karen rose and came towards me. 'I did enjoy your book launch. I'm just thankful I'd left before . . . I was so very sorry for you when I heard, it must have been awful. Did you want to see Mr Ridgeway?'

'Is that possible?'

'Officially, no, but I'll just slip in and ask if he'll see you. We've got everyone who's anyone wanting to talk to him. Mainly agents who want to audition their people for *Kids' World*, and journalists, of course. Jessica Savage has called three times already.'

Ignoring the phone which was lighting up again, she knocked on Tony's door and entered quietly. A few minutes later she came out and nodded.

'Go right in, Mr Douglas.'

'Micky! What are you doing up here?' Tony motioned me to a chair. 'What a bloody day! Don't tell me, you've been sleuthing, eh, Sherlock?'

I sat down and accepted a drink. 'Not really, Tony, just having a chat with Frank and thought I'd look in.'

'Don't try to fool me,' he chucked, 'I've known you too long. What's on your mind, mate?'

'Nothing, really,' I protested. 'I hear you're being offered all sorts of people to take Maddy's place already.'

'They'd be lucky,' he said cheerfully. 'No, I've just signed a contract with Bobby. He's the new *Kids' World* host and Angela is on her way up to the studio. She's feeling better and doesn't want to stay at home moping. I'm going to offer her a role as well. Get a whole new look, a new format. What do you say to that?'

I frowned. 'Isn't it a bit too much to expect of her? She's still at school.'

'Don't worry, she'll cope. Angela's tough—far stronger than Maddy. We'll get her a tutor, anything she needs. Heaps of kids work in the industry and go to school as well. It's what she wants and she'll love it. She's level-headed. She won't go to pieces like her mother.'

'Well, handle her gently, Tony. She's been through quite enough.'

'She'll be fine,' Tony insisted. 'We get on, Angie and I. She likes me. I'm more a father to her than Morgan was.' He grinned.

I was irritated by his attitude. 'Don't be too sure, Tony. She's not very pleased with you at the moment. She didn't like the way you and Maddy had a laugh over poor Gwen sending Maddy flowers to try and make it up with her.'

His smile faded. 'I didn't know she knew about that.'

'Well, she did and it hurt her very much. She liked Gwen a lot. If you're wise you'll be a bit tactful and not rubbish Gwen when Angie's around.'

'No, I won't. Thanks, Micky. I didn't realize I'd upset the kid.'

'I'm worried about her,' I confessed. 'Keep an eye on her, Tony. You and Becky are her closest friends now. She's all churned up about Maddy and Gwen and Bobby.'

'Ah, she's a bit keen on him, I know. Puppy love! That'll be over soon enough when they're working together. He won't seem like such a hero when they're down to the real nuts and bolts of putting a show together.'

'Perhaps you're right.'

Tony was watching me. 'What's bothering you, Micky? Come on, spit it out. How long have we known each other, eh?'

I figured he'd hear it soon enough anyway. I said awkwardly, 'Look, how well do you know Frank Young?'

'Pretty well. Why?'

'Do you think he could have killed Maddy?'

Tony jumped. 'What the hell? Gwenny killed her, you know that.'

'I know that's what everyone thinks, but suppose she didn't?'

'Come off it! She left a suicide note, plain as day.'

'But it didn't actually say she killed Maddy.'

'Not in so many words but the inference was clear.'

'Did you know Maddy had bruise marks on her throat? It looks as if there may have been two attempts on her life.'

'That's bloody ridiculous.' Tony made a dismissive gesture.

'Perhaps someone tried to strangle her and didn't realize she wasn't dead. Frank hates violence. He might have botched it. Then Gwen stabbed her later.'

'You've been watching too much television.' He laughed without humour. 'Look, just accept it. Gwen Bright said she did it by herself and that's the end of it.'

'When did she do it?' I asked. That was what had troubled me all along.

'When she said she went over to Maddy. It's obvious.'

'It can't have been then,' I objected, 'because Angela said Maddy was asleep and snoring and Bobby backed her up.'

'Angela said that?'

'Yes, didn't she tell you?'

'No, she hasn't spoken about it and we didn't like to—' He looked at me, worried. 'This puts it in a whole new light. I was sure it was Gwen—after what Maddy put her through.'

'Did Maddy ever hit Gwen?' I asked abruptly.

'Yes, she did, I'm afraid. I didn't say anything in front of Becky and Angela when the police asked, but she'd started to take her temper out on Gwen. Gwenny came to me for advice and I said she should chuck Maddy. Of course, she wouldn't. Said she couldn't abandon her after all those years. She'd feel guilty. Poor woman, no wonder she finally snapped and did the only thing left she could do.'

'But did she? What about Angela's evidence?'

'Look, I can give you two perfectly good reasons for that. One, you said yourself Angie was fond of Gwen. Supposing the poor kid saw Gwen do it and lied to cover up for her? Then, Gwen could have done it after Angie saw Maddy. Simple! Why drag poor Frank into it?'

'His story's pretty contradictory and he went missing at the time Gwen was killed. Tracey Whitehead said he had a fight with Maddy on Sunday night. A real yelling match.

She'd come back to the house for some papers and heard his voice. She told Gwen. If Gwen had given Frank any inkling that she knew, perhaps suspecting him of Maddy's murder, he could have gone to silence her, not realizing she'd already told the police.'

'Did you ask Frank about this?' Tony asked gravely.

'Yes. He denied he'd ever been at Maddy's that night. Of course, he would if it was him.'

'I just don't believe it!' Tony looked shocked.

There was a knock at the door and Karen burst in breathlessly.

'Mr Ridgeway, the News Editor just rang. Frank Young has been arrested.'

'Christ!' Tony exploded. 'It looks as if you were right!' He leaped to his feet. 'Sorry about this, Micky. Can we talk later? I'll have to see what I can do for Frank.'

'Yes, of course. I'll be at home. Let me know what happens.'

As I unlocked the Capri a voice called, 'Micky, wait a minute,' and I turned towards the staff car park. A police car waited there, its radio broadcasting a hollow message. Frank Young was hurrying towards me. I met him at the wire fence.

'Frank! They said you'd been arrested.'

'No, not yet.' He smiled grimly. 'They want me to help them with their inquiries. They've got it wrong, Micky. For God's sake, talk to Inspector Reeves. I never went to Maddy's on Sunday night but I can't prove it. I went out, you see, in the car, so I don't have an alibi. I drove around, deciding what to do. It's the truth. I know it sounds feeble but it's the truth. You've got to help me!'

CHAPTER 28

I stopped in at Riley's on my way home. Fiona greeted me warmly.

'Micky! I thought you'd never want to come near the shop again.'

I gave her a hug. 'Not likely! Are the police about?'

'They've gone for now but they've closed the garden off and we've got another function tonight. We'll have to set it up in the shop. Go down and see Dad. He's been worried about you.'

I went downstairs to the office where John and Barbara were busy at their desks. In the room next door, Don unpacked books and checked them against invoices.

'We're trying to carry on as normal,' John said, 'but the police have been here all morning.' He rubbed his eyes tiredly. 'They've been asking questions, of course. Who knew where the whisky was kept—they took the bottle with them last night—did Don see Frank Young go near Maddy Grey at all—what are they playing at, Micky? Rebecca Ridgeway rang earlier to see if we were all right, which was very good of her, and she told us Gwen Bright had confessed and killed herself.'

'There seems to be some doubt that she actually did kill Maddy or herself. Frank Young looks like the prime suspect now.'

'Hell's bells! Is that right? Well, I couldn't say I saw him go anywhere near her and Don certainly didn't.'

'The shop looks busy,' I remarked.

'Oh yes,' he said bitterly. 'Every man and his dog wants to buy a book today. We've had people coming downstairs, nosing about. It's a bloody shambles. Ghouls!' he finished angrily.

I rang David Reeves from Riley's and headed into town. At Police Headquarters I was directed to the new Homicide section and found David's office.

'Well?' He smiled at me. 'How are the little grey cells going?'

'Don't be flippant,' I reproved him. 'I saw Frank Young earlier, before Harry Andrews carted him off.'

'Ah! We haven't arrested him, you know.'

'I don't think he did it, David.'

'And why is that?'

'I don't know,' I said helplessly. 'It's just a feeling, really. His story is so typical of someone in Maddy's clutches, going around in a sick daze. I said I'd speak to you for him.'

'Yes, well I've already had Mr Ridgeway doing that.'

'I saw him, too. He said Maddy did hit Gwen Bright and Gwen confided in him. She must have hit her on Monday before the Ridgeways arrived and it was that which pushed Gwen over the edge.'

We both sat down. David swung his chair back and forth and it made a familiar squeaking sound.

'Several things,' he said at last. 'First, the marks on Mrs Grey's throat couldn't have been caused by an attempted strangulation or, if they were, it was an incredibly amateurish attempt and wouldn't have caused unconsciousness. There was no internal damage at all and the windpipe was intact. George Thengalis tells me they're more consistent with someone pushing or forcing her head back. They were inflicted shortly before she was killed. Second, Miss Bright didn't commit suicide. She was knocked unconscious by a blow to the temple, carried to her car and arranged to look as if she'd taken her own life.'

'But the note,' I began.

'Yes, certainly an admission of guilt. We had it checked by Forensics and a handwriting expert.'

'And?' I could see he was leading up to something.

'It's definitely Miss Bright's handwriting and only her fingerprints were on it.'

'There you are, then!' I said.

'The top of the note had been cut. A nice, neat edge. By the look of her other stationery it had lost half an inch.'

'She started it, changed her mind about what she wanted to say, cut off the top and tried again.'

'And the missing piece magically disappeared,' David said ironically. 'We searched for it, naturally. It wasn't in the house.'

'Oh! Perhaps someone removed it.'

'Why?'

I thought. 'Well, if there was only one attempt on Maddy's life, Gwen either did it or she saw who did. If someone else did, they found out that she saw them, killed her and removed the top of the note.' I felt quite proud of myself.

'Why?' David asked again.

'Er—it was addressed to him—or her?'

'Doesn't make sense.'

I knew he was testing me but I couldn't make it out. 'Anyway,' I said, thoroughly confused, 'if she didn't do it, why was she writing a confession at all?'

'Exactly!' David looked pleased. There was a tap on the door and Sergeant Hobbs came in.

'He's just left, sir.'

'Good.' David turned to me. 'Let me set your mind at rest. Frank Young is once again a free man.'

'I thought—' I began, but he silenced me with a look.

'Micky, you've been talking to people today. Now you're going to talk to me. I want everything this time, no matter how trivial.' I swallowed. Sergeant Hobbs grinned sympathetically and closed the door. I faced the two Homicide detectives. I hadn't a clue what they wanted. David pulled a pad forward and looked at me.

'Let's have it, Micky. All of it!'

It was well over an hour before they let me go. I went home in a sober mood. It was the second time I'd been on the receiving end of one of David's interrogations and he hadn't missed a thing. Talking it out had focused my mind and I was thinking clearly for the first time in weeks. And what I was thinking sickened me. David still hadn't said, in so many words, who he suspected but, as Tony had said, the inference was clear.

I turned up the volume control on the answering machine as soon as I got in. Something told me I needed to hear the calls, no matter what. As the afternoon dragged on I felt a depression settling on me. A walk, I thought, around the park and back. But I couldn't leave the flat. A premonition? Finally, ignoring David's warning to stay out of it, I picked up the phone and dialled.

Jessica was still at the paper. She answered briskly.

'Michael. Any more news?'

'No,' I said baldly, 'I want to ask you something, Jess. About your column a couple of weeks ago.' I continued to talk, ignoring the uncooperative silence at the other end.

When I wound to a halt she said coolly, 'Nothing about this is any of your business, Michael.'

'I know, but it's important, Jess. You've kept it a secret all these years which tells me more about you than you'd care to admit.'

'I don't have to say anything,' she said, but she sounded shaken.

'It's all going to come out,' I told her. 'This thing isn't over yet and that's the key to it.'

'You're taking a risk. This is big news. Suppose I just go ahead and publish?'

'You could have done that at the beginning. You didn't for Morgan's sake and you won't do it now. I trust you for that.'

'Then you're a fool!' she said angrily. 'And Morgan was a bigger one.' I thought she was crying. Then she said urgently, 'Michael, wait. Something's coming in. Oh my God!'

I waited as the minutes ticked by, wondering what was keeping her. At last she came back and said quickly, 'There's been another murder. Tracey Whitehead. Someone broke into her flat and stabbed her to death!'

After Jessica had hurriedly rung off I sat for a long time, just staring at the phone. When it suddenly rang I jumped out of my skin and waited a moment, listening to its shrill demand for attention. Then, reluctantly, I picked up the receiver.

'Micky?' David said tersely. 'There's been another death. Mrs Grey's secretary, Miss Whitehead. She's been stabbed.'

I swallowed. David said, 'Micky? Are you still there?'

'Yes.' My voice was tired. 'I already knew, David. Jessica Savage just told me.'

'We were on our way there, after we talked to you,' David went on. 'We realized she was in danger. We were too late.'

'Frank?' I asked.

'He's at the studio. Micky, leave this to us. I don't want you getting involved.'

'I am involved,' I said harshly. 'These people are my friends. Do you think I'm going to sit back and do nothing, knowing they're still in danger?'

'We've got a car on the way to Channel 6,' David said. 'I'm warning you, Micky, keep out of it.'

I felt a blinding anger surging through me. 'You can't stop me,' I told David. 'I'm a private citizen and I'm not under arrest. I can go where I like and talk to whoever I damn well please.'

'There's such a thing as obstructing the police,' David said curtly. 'If I have to get heavy, I'll do it.'

But I'd hung up. God knows what I thought I could do that David and his men couldn't but I was past listening to reason. I felt used and betrayed and knew my hurt was as much for Morgan as for myself. I poured myself a drink, my hand only slightly shaking.

'Don't worry, mate,' I told Morgan's memory. 'I'll see justice is done, you can count on it.' But I didn't have any clear idea of what I was going to do. Just talk, as I'd told David? Or was I once again succumbing to the urge that most women of my acquaintance have no difficulty recognizing? I was trying to work out a plan of attack when the phone shrilled again.

'Yes?' I snapped.

'Micky? It's Tony. Are you OK?'

My nerves jumped to attention. 'Yes, sorry, Tony. What's up?'

He sounded seriously worried. 'The police have just been here. You'd better sit down, Micky. They've arrested Bobby West and Angela.'

'What!' I exploded.

'God's truth! Are they completely mad? They've taken them into custody. It's got to be a mistake, hasn't it? Christ, they're my two stars! Are those bastards trying to ruin me?' He was a broken man. 'I just don't believe those two were involved.'

'Tony, Tracey Whitehead's been murdered.'

'Yeah, I know. It's a bloody awful situation, but they can't think Angie—and Bobby? It's ludicrous!'

'They're doing what they have to do,' I said feebly. 'I don't understand it either but they must have evidence.'

'Look, can I talk to you? I could come around—say in about half an hour? Perhaps together we can get it sorted. You're a mate of the Inspector. He might listen to you.'

I thought rapidly, changing my plans for now.

'Sure, Tony,' I told him. 'I've got nothing else on at the moment. Come on down.'

CHAPTER 29

Tony slumped on to the sofa like a man at the end of his tether and took out his cigarettes.

'Mind if I smoke?'

Usually No.5 is a non-smoking zone but he looked desperate, so I dug out an ashtray.

'Go ahead, Tony. I've put a pot of coffee on—thought you could use it.' I went into the kitchenette and nearly closed the door on Carnie, who followed me in with an amazed look.

'What *is* going on?' she said plainly. 'I hope all this isn't going to interfere with my dinner!'

'Sorry, Princess.' I turned off the hotplate and poured the coffee. 'You stay in here and keep hoping.'

'Did you ring the Inspector?' Tony asked anxiously as I returned.

'Yes. He said to tell you he has his reasons.'

Tony thumped the sofa, making my nerves twitch. 'He can't run around arresting people like this.'

'I'd rather have thought he could,' I said drily.

'Ah!' Tony looked at me closely. 'Not so friendly with Reeves these days?'

'We had a difference of opinion earlier,' I told him stiffly. 'He threatened me with obstructing the police.'

'God, the man's a little Hitler,' Tony burst out angrily. 'What's the story about the kids?'

'He said he's brought them in for questioning and he expects to make an arrest before the day's out.'

'Well, I don't believe it and no one will convince me they're implicated.'

'It doesn't seem likely,' I agreed, 'but look at the facts, Tony.'

'Eh? What bloody facts?' He put down his cup and stared at me.

'It was their testimony after the launch. You see, they both gave each other away pretty obviously. Angela had told Bobby she was going to see Maddy but she went upstairs, thinking Maddy was still there. Bobby decided to make sure everything was OK, knowing how Maddy's temper was, and he went to Maddy himself, thinking Angela had already seen her. At that point, Angela was asking you where her mother was and she saw Bobby leave the dark corner. Then she went over.'

'Well, so what?' Tony was impatient.

'When they told their stories to Reeves, Angela said she'd found Maddy asleep. When David pressed her she embroidered her statement. Not only was Maddy asleep but she was snoring loudly.'

'That sounds like the truth to me.'

'Oh yes, completely plausible, except no one else heard Maddy. The police checked with everyone. Now, Bobby also made an obvious slip. He said Maddy was asleep and making movements and muttering. When David mentioned that Angela had heard Maddy snoring Bobby immediately said he'd heard her too. It was clearly a lie to back Angela up. When he was told Angela hadn't gone to Maddy until after he himself had seen her, he was enormously relieved.'

'I don't get it,' Tony said slowly. 'What are you saying?'

'I'm saying that their stories suggest they were giving each other alibis. That when Angela saw Maddy she was already dead and Angela thought Bobby had killed her. Angela loves Bobby rather more than you supposed. She was willing to lie to protect him. Then Bobby agreed with her story. Later on each was trying to reassure the other, saying everything would be all right. I think they were trying to indicate that each had made it OK with the police.'

'You think Bobby did kill Maddy?'

'Who else could have done it?'

'But Gwenny—she confessed. She did it.'

'No,' I said gently, 'Gwen didn't do it. She was unlucky enough to see the real killer and she also lied to protect him —or her. And so she in turn was killed.'

'I can think of only one person Gwen would have protected,' Tony said reluctantly, 'and that's Angela.'

'Or someone Angela loved,' I agreed, 'which once again points to Bobby—unless you can think of anyone else who could have killed Maddy.'

'But why did Gwen confess?' Tony asked helplessly.

'She didn't, of course,' I said. 'That wasn't a confession of murder but a confession of guilt. Maddy was furious with Gwen for interfering in her daughter's career—because of your prompting her, Tony. When Maddy sacked her, Gwen was so heartbroken that she sent Maddy a bunch of flowers with a note. She knew if Maddy found out you'd been behind her support of Angela, she'd have cut you, too, and ruined herself. Gwen loved Maddy and knew just how much she needed *Kids' World*. So in her note she claimed full responsibility for her actions. That was the note the police found. The murderer knew about it, had seen it earlier and realized it would make an excellent suicide note if the top was trimmed off. The top half-inch that said something like, "Dear Maddy".'

Tony looked aghast. 'Angela knew about that note,' he said. 'You told me. But she couldn't have killed Gwen. She was at home with Becky and me all night.'

'She could have told Bobby about it,' I reminded him. 'If she and Bobby were in league.'

'Christ!' Tony sat back helplessly.

'In fact, I can only think of one thing which could knock holes in David's case against Angela and Bobby.'

'Well, let's have it.' Tony jerked himself up again excitedly.

'Frank Young,' I said.

'Of course! I was forgetting Frank. Tracey overheard him having a fight with Maddy and now Tracey's dead, too.'

'Yes, and within an hour of Frank's being released by the police.'

'That's right! Wait!' He frowned in urgent thought. 'Frank kills Maddy. Gwenny sees him and he knows it. He kills Gwen to shut her up but it's too late. The police already know about the row with Maddy. Then he talks to you.' Tony looked at me and repeated slowly. 'He talks to you, Micky. He probably didn't know about Tracey coming back to the house until then. But you told him and he killed her.'

'Yes,' I said quietly. 'I'm very aware that it was my fault Tracey was killed. I'll never be able to forget it and the only reparation I can make is to bring her killer to justice. It's not much in exchange for a life but it's better than sitting back and letting a cold-blooded murderer go free.'

'Be careful, mate,' Tony warned me. 'Frank's killed three times already. If he thinks you're likely to shop him he won't hesitate to have a go at you.'

'I know it,' I said. 'I could be in danger this very minute.'

'Well, hardly.' Tony grinned. 'I'm here with you.'

'True,' I said, 'but I can't cart you around with me all day.'

'You could ask for police protection. When I've gone.'

'They've got enough to do. But you know, Tony, when I said Frank was the only person who could ruin the case against Angela and Bobby, I meant his evidence after the launch.'

'What was that?' He looked interested.

'He pointed quite clearly to the time of death.' I let that sink in and watched Tony thinking it through.

'You'd better explain,' he said. 'I must be slow today.'

'You heard him yourself,' I reminded him. 'Frank said she was cool to the touch. He said it again later, to David.'

'Of course she was,' Tony said, puzzled. 'She was dead.'

'But if Bobby or Angela had killed her it could only have been after the launch. And she couldn't have been killed that late. She wouldn't have lost heat in that time. She had to have been killed earlier. Of course, Bobby had already given that away.'

'How, for God's sake?'

'Maddy was already dead when he saw her,' I told him calmly, 'which is why he got so confused in his evidence. He went to Maddy, thinking Angela had already seen her. He found her dead and immediately jumped to the conclusion Angela had done it. So he told an obvious lie to protect her. When he found out she'd gone to Maddy after himself he said, "That's all right, then," meaning it couldn't have been Angela. So it's fairly clear Maddy was already dead. Of course, he didn't realize Angie could still have killed her after Bobby had seen her but Frank's evidence takes care of that, anyway. That was why Angela didn't try to wake Maddy herself. She already knew she was dead. When David asked her why she hadn't gone home when you suggested it, she said, "I don't run out on people when they're in trouble." We thought she meant Maddy, but she meant Bobby, of course. They caused a lot of confusion claiming Maddy was still alive but it'll all be sorted now. So someone else must have killed Maddy—and a good deal earlier.'

'Gwen!' Tony exclaimed. 'I thought you were coming back to her.'

I touched my cup. It was stone cold but I didn't want to go back into the kitchen. I hoped Tony wouldn't ask for a refill.

'Yes, but don't forget, Tracey was killed after Gwen was dead.'

'You said there could be two people, two attempts on Maddy's life,' he pointed out.

'Oh, didn't I tell you? That theory fell through. Those weren't strangulation marks. It looks more as if someone forced Maddy's head back really hard for some reason, earlier in the evening.'

'That could've been Gwen, too,' he said eagerly, 'when she went to Maddy's before the launch.'

'Why on earth would she do such a thing?'

'They must have had another fight. Perhaps Maddy hit her and she shoved Maddy's head back.'

'There is, of course, one other person who could have done it,' I mused, 'and a hell of a good case against him.'

Tony stared. 'Who's that?' he asked.

'It's you, Tony,' I said.

CHAPTER 30

Tony gave a shout of laughter. 'Oh, great!' he said. 'You really had me going there. Stop trying to be funny, Micky.'

'I'm deadly serious, Tony.'

His smile faded. 'You are, aren't you? Come on, Micky. When was I supposed to have done it?'

'When you brought Maddy down.'

'Well, that's bloody ridiculous because Gwenny herself said Maddy was alive when she saw her and that was after I left her.'

'How did you know that?' I asked.

He stared at me. 'You told me.'

'No, no, I didn't, Tony. Only the police and I knew that.'

'Oh, look, this is going too far. Gwen must have told me.'

'When?' I asked. 'You only spoke a few words to her after the launch and Constable Bates recorded those.'

'Ah! I've just remembered. Inspector Reeves told me.'

'No, he didn't. I was there. He just said Gwen had gone over to Maddy after you left her.'

'You're bloody mad.' His face flushed. 'You can't think I

had anything to do with it. I needed Maddy. Do you think
I'd kill the star of my show?'

'Oh yes, I'm sure of it. I can prove it was you, you know.'

'All right, I'll humour you.' He sat back with an amused
look. 'I told you, you've been watching too much TV. Who
do you think you are? Columbo? You just tell me how I
killed Maddy—and, while you're at it, why I'd want to—
and Gwen, oh, and Tracey, of course.'

'I think you'd been wanting to be rid of Maddy for a
long time,' I said evenly. 'I should have guessed earlier
because you practically told me so yourself. She was becoming unstable and unpredictable and was placing the show
in serious jeopardy. Not only that, you wanted some new
blood in *Kids' World* but Maddy wouldn't hear of Angela
and I wouldn't let you have Winifred. I think you'd decided
to get rid of Maddy and replace her with Bobby and Angela.
You said as much when I went to see you. So you hit on a
perfect way. You'd push Maddy over the edge, get her even
more hooked into alcohol and use the unreliability clause
to put her out. You told me you'd suggested trying Angela
in *Kids' World* and Maddy got hysterical. You said you
should have known better. Hell, Tony, you did know better.
In fact, you knew exactly how Maddy would react. You
encouraged Angela and manipulated Gwen, always driving
Maddy further into a desperate state. It was calculating
and deliberate and it makes me sick to think about it. You
pushed her to the bottle, knowing what would happen.

'Stop!' He was taut with anger. 'Even supposing I did
all that, why should I have killed her? I could have had her
thrown out at any time, the way she was behaving.'

'I'm sure you would have,' I agreed, 'except for one
thing. Maddy had a secret. A secret that she threatened to
use to destroy you. She hinted to Becky many times that
there was something between you two. Becky ignored her,
thinking it was just Maddy being catty. I don't believe you

knew about it yourself until one day you pushed Maddy too far and she told you.'

His face was beginning to show the strain. 'I don't know what you're talking about but I'm sure you'll come up with some extraordinary fantasy out of that head of yours.'

'Not so extraordinary,' I said sadly. 'Rather ordinary and sordid, really. I confirmed it with Jessica earlier. In spite of all your protestations about what good mates you and Morgan were, you'd had an affair with Maddy yourself. Back at the very beginning. She made a play for you and you let it go all the way.'

'You can't prove that.'

'I don't need to. There's living proof. Angela Grey isn't Morgan's daughter. She's yours.'

'No!' He spat out the word.

'I think yes. Jess knew you were sleeping with Maddy. She hinted in her column about a producer and said Becky deserved all the good she could get but she didn't know it. Rather an odd thing to say. But you made an odd slip yourself. When David was questioning you, you said, when Maddy wanted to sue Jessica for libel, that it wasn't libel, she was telling the truth. Then you said, "If *I* didn't—" and changed it to "If I told her once I told her a dozen times." The inflection puzzled me. I think you were about to say something like, "If I didn't mind, why should she?" It made me think you'd been the producer in question. And, of course, you joined *Kids' World* just a year before Angela was born. Jessica could've destroyed Maddy if she'd published that story—but she was in love with Morgan. She still is. She'd never have exposed him. She told me she was sure Angela wasn't Morgan's child. He was so dark and she's so fair, like Maddy—and like you, Tony. Angela's said to me more than once that she wished she'd taken after her father in colouring. Poor kid. That's exactly what she did do.'

He smiled but it was a sickly attempt. 'Sheer fantasy. Have you thought of writing romance?'

'I don't find much romance in this story. I think when you pushed Maddy too far she told you the truth. Angela was your child and she'd tell the world and wreck your marriage and career, if she could. But it backfired on her, didn't it? Because suddenly she'd dealt you the very ace you wanted. If Angela was your daughter, you had a say in her career. If you could prove Maddy an unfit mother, Angela would be yours. I wondered why, when you first talked about getting her into *Kids' World*, you said you'd need Maddy's signature on the contract, then suddenly you said you had her father's permission. A dead man's arrangements wouldn't have counted against a living mother's wishes. But if you were the father—you see? It was suddenly obvious.'

'Still no reason to kill Maddy. It seems I had it all my way.'

'Not if she talked. You went to see Maddy on Sunday night—but you didn't go away leaving her all smiles as you suggested. No, you had a row with her about Angela. She threatened that if you didn't do exactly what she wanted she'd tell the truth about you being Angela's father. And you told her you'd stop her any way you had to. Tracey Whitehead came back for some papers she'd left behind the day before and she overheard you.'

'You're confused,' he said coolly. 'Tracey overheard Maddy and Frank. And you told me that yourself.'

'That's what she thought. It was a natural mistake. Frank had an appointment with Maddy but he never kept it. So his name was in her appointment book and Tracey saw it. When she overheard the fight, through a closed door, she assumed it was Frank because she expected Frank —and your voices are extremely alike. Even David noticed the similarity. Both deep and well trained—actors' voices —or announcers.'

'I suppose I can't convince you it wasn't me.'

'I'm not the one you'll need to convince. But no. Why would Maddy have been talking about Frank and Morgan? They'd never met. For a brief moment I jumped to quite another conclusion, because of something Frank said—but then I realized the truth.'

'Well, this is all fascinating,' Tony said, 'but really, Micky, who's going to believe it?'

'David Reeves, for one,' I told him. 'You see, you're the only possible suspect for Maddy's death. You had motive —you had to shut her up before she destroyed you—and you had the best opportunity.'

'I suppose you're going to tell me how I did it?'

'I think I can,' I agreed. 'You made a great show of sobering Maddy up. Then you got rid of the Rileys and Gwen and told them that you'd stay with Maddy and bring her down. Jess heard you arguing with her. We assumed she'd got cold feet and didn't want to do the launch and you were trying to talk her round. I think you were actually trying to stop her exposing you. Then, in desperation, you took the whisky bottle out. You knew where it was kept. John Riley told me you'd dropped in and had a drink with him and told him you were upset about Maddy's proposed move to Channel 8. If you'd killed Maddy in the office everyone would have known it was you. So you forced back her head so hard you bruised her throat—and you poured half the bottle into her. That was how she got so drunk. She couldn't have known where to find the bottle and anyway, she wanted to be sober enough to make that speech.

'Then you came out and told your story. I don't think you meant to kill her. I think you were just trying to shut her up until you could reason with her. You thought she'd be out like a light until after the launch, and she would have been if she'd been left alone. But of course, Gillian Fry went to see her. Poor Gilly didn't know what Maddy was saying and thought she was being deliberately provocative. But Maddy, deep in a drunken stupor, was capable of only one thought. She accused Gilly of going behind her back, influencing her daughter. She said she'd expose her. She was still following on her argument with you but she'd been disturbed enough to start coming around.

'Then Fiona Riley tried to talk to her and woke her up fully. Maddy remembered what she had to do. She staggered out of the office, right into your arms. She wanted to launch the book, you said. She felt guilty. But Jessica, who was close enough to hear, said Maddy was talking about "Angela's precious father" and exposing something. She also thought it must be about Morgan. Then you told Maddy you'd let her get it off her chest. Quite a different conversation from the one you reported. I think you realized then you'd never be able to silence her in the future—unless you did it in the only way you could be sure. You'd always been able to handle her but suddenly you'd lost your touch. She was too far gone with all the hatred and alcohol abuse.

'You'd noticed the ice pick earlier. Now you sat Maddy down, got her a drink and slipped the ice pick in your pocket. You drugged Maddy first. Then you stabbed her. If suspicion fell on you, you could say, "I drugged her— why would I then stab her?" which we'd all been thinking. You went back to the table and carefully, under the pretext of getting yourself a drink, you washed the pick in the ice bucket which had enough melted water in the bottom, then dropped it in a box under the table to make it look as if it had slipped off. You knew there'd be blood in the bucket so you overturned it. You got your sleeve wet, which Frank noticed. Then you went back and acted normally.'

'Bravo!' he applauded. 'It's wonderful. No wonder you're a writer. I thought we knew each other better than this, Micky. I always thought you were my friend.'

'I thought so too,' I said, 'but you lied to me from the beginning and used me as you used everyone. Poor Gwen. She went to Maddy just after you'd left her dead. She realized it had to be you. She was seen staring at you oddly. Then she thought, perhaps if she protected you, you'd look after her. It was blackmail, wasn't it? She appeared totally cut up about Maddy but she was faking it. I guessed it but I didn't know why. She must have already been calculating how to make sure she'd come off all right. She told the police Maddy was alive. The only way you could have known that is if you'd seen her and the only time you could have seen her was before she was killed. Before you killed her.'

CHAPTER 31

He'd forgotten to smile. 'Go on,' he said, 'let's hear the rest of this.'

I was watching him as closely as I dared, waiting for the end. 'You reassured Gwen as you were leaving,' I said carefully. 'You thanked her for not saying anything about Maddy. You meant for not giving you away. She said she didn't know what to do and you'd have to advise her. You knew exactly what she was asking. You told her what she wanted to hear, that she'd be all right. You took Angela and Becky home and waited until you thought Gwen would be at her house. You sent Becky to sleep with Angela so you'd be free to move around, then you took the car out. The noise disturbed Becky. She told me the cars seemed loud. She didn't realize it was you. You went to Gwen's and you knocked her out with a blow on the temple. Later you tried to cover it by saying Maddy had hit Gwen. You left the note, carried Gwen to the garage and left the car engine running.'

'There's one flaw there,' he broke in harshly. 'This note I was supposed to have. In Gwen's handwriting? Perhaps you'll tell me how it came to be in my possession?'

'You'd had it all along. Angela wasn't the only one who knew about the note. Maddy had showed it to you and you'd joked about it. You must have taken it then—perhaps to have a laugh at Gwen. It'd be your style. Then you realized how it could be used. You cut off the opening words, "Dear Maddy," and left it for the police to find. You'd know enough to wipe it clean of your fingerprints and Maddy's and press Gwen's fingers on to it. Even a child knows that, these days.'

'And supposing I say I never had the note?'

'I wouldn't believe you. You see, I happen to know you never saw Gwen's so-called "suicide" letter. David showed it to me but no one showed it to you or discussed its contents. I asked David because it struck me as odd at the time.'

'What was odd?' He was leaning back casually, a hand in his pocket, the epitome of a man taking his ease, but I caught the sound of danger in his voice.

'When I saw you at the studio earlier you knew what was in that note. I said it didn't say she killed Maddy and you said, "not in so many words but the inference was clear." How could you have known that, Tony, unless you'd seen the letter yourself?'

'Ah!' He sat very still, his mind going at full speed behind his eyes. 'I have to say you've got me there, Micky. Perhaps you're not as stupid as I thought.'

'I can't tell you,' I said wearily. 'I don't know how stupid that is.'

'Oh, very stupid,' he said kindly, 'which was a mistake, I admit. You've been an unending source of trouble to me with your bloody wombat and your morals and your interfering. Although I have to thank you for one thing. You tipped me off about Tracey. I knew it was only a matter of time before Frank convinced the police he hadn't been there and someone put two and two together. I couldn't afford to have Tracey tell her story and I'm afraid I can't afford to have you tell yours.'

He brought his hand out of his pocket and I found myself staring at a small blue metal pistol. I stayed very carefully put. He definitely had the advantage and he knew it.

'I came prepared, you see,' he said conversationally, 'but I wanted to find out how much you knew. You talk too much, Micky. If you'd stayed shtum I wouldn't have had to kill you.'

'And after me?' I asked him, my throat dry. 'Are you going to kill Frank to stop him talking, and Angela and Bobby? And Jessica? Get real, Tony. The police will be on to you like a shot.' I winced. There'd been no pun intended but he laughed anyway.

'Well said. But do you think I care? I'm finished anyway. It'll be a pleasure to take you with me.' He stood up. 'You were right, about all of it. Christ knows how you did it, but you were right.' He came towards me and I knew I was looking death in the face.

'It's a shame,' he said, and he actually sounded regretful. 'We had some good times. Maddy wasn't worth all this. She was a little tart. Morgan knew but he didn't bloody care.'

'Morgan was a good man,' I said quietly. 'He knew Maddy, as you say. He must have suspected Angela wasn't his daughter, he must have known about you and Maddy. He didn't miss a trick. But he was man enough to accept Angela—to love her—and to remain the truest friend you ever had, Tony.'

'He was a bloody fool!' Tony shouted. 'Don't tell me what a saint he was. If he'd been a real man he'd have put a stop to Maddy's games and not let her suck the poor bastards in. You think he was some sort of hero? You were never in Maddy's clutches. What made you so bloody perfect? Well, take a good look around, Mr-Bloody-Wonderful, because this is the last thing you're going to see.'

I watched, fascinated, as the gun drew level with my heart. There was nowhere I could go. I took a deep breath.

The kitchen door opened with a bang. Tony jumped and spun around just a fraction too late. Harry Andrews had him pinned against the wall in seconds, Brian Hobbs took the gun and carefully engaged the safety-catch.

David Reeves faced Tony and his voice was like ice. 'Anthony James Ridgeway, I'm arresting you for the murder of Madeline Grey. You are not obliged to say anything unless you wish to do so, but anything you do say will be put into writing and may be given in evidence.'

Tony sagged at the knees and stared past David at me. 'You bastard!' he spat. 'I'll deny every bloody thing.'

'I'm afraid your conversation was taped,' David said and pulled a sofa cushion aside to reveal the police machine still recording the action, thank goodness. Tony gave a frustrated howl and lunged at me but the sergeants held him back.

'Get him out of here, Harry,' David snapped. As the door closed behind them he turned to me.

'Well?' he said.

I grinned. '*Thank* you, David.'

'Bloody idiot.' David gripped my hand. 'We could have got him without this.'

'I owed Morgan,' I said quietly, 'and Tracey. If I hadn't gone to Tony and shot my mouth off, she'd still be alive.'

'But Angela Grey and Bobby West might very well have been dead. Once he started removing people he thought were in his way, he wouldn't have stopped. Murder can very quickly develop into a habit.'

'What about Angela and Bobby?'

'We called Mrs Ridgeway. She's with them at the station. We thought it best to keep them until they were out of danger. Once Ridgeway was told they'd known Mrs Grey was dead they were obvious candidates for his list. After you, that is.' He smiled at me. 'You did well, Micky.'

I was surprised. I'd expected a lecture on the non-interference of the private citizen in police affairs.

CHAPTER 32

Two days later the Rileys and I were sitting around the table on the bookshop's back verandah. It was an hour after closing time and the dusk had begun to settle quietly on the steep, terraced garden below. I came to the end of my story and sat back, sipping my wine. I'd been invited for a celebratory drink but they still hadn't told me what we were celebrating.

'Later,' John had said. 'We want your news first.'

Barbara shook her head sadly. 'Poor Tony,' she said. 'One can understand—but then to go on a killing spree simply to silence anyone who could expose him—that was a dreadful thing.'

'The only decent thing he did was to hold on to Angela so she wouldn't run to Maddy—and he tried to get her to leave with Bobby so she'd be spared the shock of the discovery. He didn't know she'd already found her mother dead.'

'And she was dead when I saw her.' Fiona shuddered. 'I never realized. I thought she was asleep. I didn't go close enough to notice anything was wrong.'

John had been silent throughout the story but now he stirred. 'Poor bugger! No wonder he looked so done in after the launch. He took a fearful risk, leaving Maddy where anyone could find her. He must have been expecting her to be discovered at any moment.'

'He had no choice,' I said. 'He had to establish an alibi and allow the time span so it was possible one of the others had done it. He couldn't hang around stopping anyone going over there—that would have looked suspicious. And, once the launch was under way he knew people would stay where they were and keep their attention on the gazebo, so all he had to do was stand in a conspicuous place and act normally. He didn't see Gwen go to Maddy and he'd advised Angela to leave her alone until it was all over, so he felt he'd be safe for a while. But after the speeches he would have been waiting minute by minute for someone to find her.'

'I thought the Inspector had decided Fi and I did it,' Don said soberly. 'Especially after I washed up the evidence.'

'David was suspicious of Tony from the first,' I told him, 'simply because he'd been alone with Maddy and she'd obviously been given alcohol. He's not stupid.'

'What about Angela?' Fiona asked quietly. 'It's awful for her.'

'I went to see her earlier,' I said. 'She's bearing up surprisingly well. She and Bobby had a long talk with Becky about their future. Becky's going to look after Angela. She's decided to leave *Summer Days* and go into the production side. She'll be producing *Kids' World*. Angela won't be going into the show yet. She said she wants to get away for a while. She's asked Becky to follow up on Maddy's idea of sending her to a school in the country.'

'But Bobby,' Fi protested.

'She thinks it's better to not see him for a while. She's right, you know. Angela needs time to grow up, go out with other boys, find her feet emotionally. She'll see him in the holidays, of course. If they still feel the same way about each other in a few years' time, then they'll talk about it again. Angela still wants a career in television, but she's leaning towards scriptwriting.' I smiled modestly. 'She says that's my influence.'

There was a shout and we all turned towards the sound. On the verandah of the antique shop next door stood a familiar figure, waving a bottle.

'Ahoy there, John, open your door and let me in.'

John ran upstairs and returned with a triumphant Henri Piccard.

'It is done, accomplished! We are in business, my friends!'

Fiona and Barbara leaped to their feet, Fi squealing with delight. Don took the bottle and opened it.

'Champagne,' Henri announced. 'French, of course.' He held up his glass. 'We drink success to the Rileys and Henri Piccard, yes?'

We did. 'Although I haven't the faintest idea why,' I said.

Henri turned to me. 'After you left the other day I began to think about my situation and the poor Rileys. I had been looking for new premises and I was aware the owner of this shop and the one next door was wishing to sell. I thought: There are the Rileys, always having this function and that and drawing much custom, but rents are high, costs are high, they struggle. And, at the other end of Paddington, there am I, Henri Piccard, superb restaurateur, where people drop in for dinner or supper after a Riley affair. This is ridiculous, I thought. We could save them the trouble by being closer together. So I made inquiries.' He nodded at John.

'Henri came to see me,' John explained, 'with a proposition. He's got the money but not enough customers. I've got the customers and no money! So Henri suggested he buy both places and open his restaurant next door.'

'Not just next door,' Barbara said. 'We're going to put a walkway through so people can come to browse among the books and then have a cup of coffee together. We've always wanted to do that but there's not the space in the shop.'

'So, just now, I finalized the deal.' Henri was flushed with enthusiasm. 'We will have a coffee lounge upstairs in the antique shop, a restaurant downstairs and a terraced garden, like this one, with outdoor dining perhaps—but, at least, a delightful place for the diners to sit or stroll. I will cater for the Rileys' functions and their rent will go to paying off their shop so one day they will own it outright. It is a good scheme, no?'

'Brilliant!' I smiled around at their excited faces. 'I'm so pleased for you all.'

'We'll do the literary lunches at Henri's as well,' Don added. 'It couldn't be better, really.'

'No, it couldn't be better. I smiled to myself as I drove home. Things had worked out for me, as well. I had a contract in my pocket which gave *Kids' World* the television rights to Winifred. Becky was going to make my wombat a star—what Winifred had always wanted, in fact.

I hadn't told the Rileys that Tony was Angela's real father. I'd finally told Becky and she'd made the painful decision to tell Angela. Angela had listened quietly and had taken the news with characteristic calm.

'I don't really remember Morgan,' she'd explained simply, 'but I'd rather think of him as my dad and let the world think so, too. Can it be kept quiet, about Mum and Tony?'

'Yes, David will see to it,' I assured her.

She'd hugged me. 'I think you mind more than I do,' she said suddenly. 'I'll be all right, Micky.'

I ran the Capri into my parking space outside No. 18 and sat for a moment, staring across the park opposite. A new moon hung silver in the sky and the mopoke, annoyed at having been disturbed, hooted at me crossly. The harsh chatter of the possum sounded as he headed across next door's roof on his way to our compost heap and a dust-up with next door's cat, if it was around.

There was a hum of traffic from the main road but otherwise the night was quiet with only a whisper of wind in the trees.

I looked up at the flats and noticed a light at No. 4, Peta Ryde's place. I shook myself. Of course, Peta had been due back today. I locked the car and let myself in at the front door. Peta would want to tell me all about her trip and she'd have taken dozens of photographs. I had my own story to tell her, which would mean Carnie and I would be invited for dinner and then, who could say.

Whistling, I ran up the stairs.